AP

GL

VOLUME III:
THE FESTIVES

By Jamie RJ Richmond

Best Wishes

Jamie RJ

1

WARNING: THIS BOOK
CONTAINS SWEARING
AND ADULT THEMES

AND IS STRICTLY

<u>NOT</u> FOR CHILDREN.

For all of my family,

who made every holiday

and festivity,

the best that it could be.

CHAPTER 1

THE STORKS

A perfectly good afternoon in South Shields was completely ruined as Harry Stork pulled his brand-new Citroen C4 Cactus into his immaculate looking drive and noticed the bird shit sprayed across his garage door.

"You've got to be kidding me?" Harry raged, getting out of his car for a closer look.

The father looked around suspiciously at all of the birds that sat on the different roofs of the estate, as if trying to work out which particular crow did it. Suddenly, he spotted one on the grass beside his home pecking for worms. He aimed a boot at the bird but it was too fast for him and it flew away.

"Knob." He thought he heard the bird shout before it flew off, landing on a neighbour's guttering alongside another two crows.

"I'm sick of these birds, I'm gonna complain to the council and get this group shifted." Harry promised as he got back into the car with his wife and two children.

"Murder." His fifteen-year-old son Samuel noted.

"I will murder them alright." He said pulling the car into the garage.

"No, a group of crows is called a murder." Samuel informed.

"I don't care what they're called or what they do for that matter, as long as they stop doing it 'round here." Harry informed as he stopped the car and lifted the hand brake.

Samuel got out first and marched straight through the side door and upstairs out of the way. His nine-year-old little sister Sophie hung back to help with the shopping.

"Can we have turkey dinosaurs for tea please?" She asked as she spotted a pack through one of the thin-looking orange shopping bags.

"No, not tonight honey." Her Mum Stephanie noted, grabbing as many bags as she could carry. Her floral dress floating behind her as she struggled after her daughter with six heavy bags.

"We will have them tomorrow." Her Dad shouted through to them before grabbing the rest of the bags and closing the boot with his chin, shoulder and then his foot.

As Sophie and her mam put the shopping away Harry began to clean the garage door with an old rag and some WD40. His son Samuel watched him through his upstairs bedroom window, heavy-rock music blasting through his expensive-looking headphones.

After a repetitive tea of spaghetti hoops, garlic baguette and turkey drummers, Samuel went straight back into his bedroom to listen to music again.

On the roof opposite his house, the three crows were now stood watching him through his bedroom window.

"It's all he ever does, listen to music." One of the crows said.

"He will end up hard of hearing that kid will." The second one noted.

"He is just a kid, discovering some of the greatest artists of all time." The third crow sympathised.

As the third crow finished his sentence a grey car pulled in beside the house.

"What do we have here?" The first crow worried as an obese man in a matching grey tracksuit got out of the car and walked to the front door.

The plump man pressed the buzzer and waited patiently for an answer.

"What do we do? What do we do?" The second crow began to panic.

"Chill out Barry, it could be anyone." The third crow assured.

The three crows watched on in anticipation as Harry answered the door and began speaking to the mystery man.

"I bet it's the council." The first crow guessed.

The pair of them chatted for about a minute before Harry looked like he was about to close the door on the man. But he didn't have a chance as the obese man pulled out a shotgun and fired a shot directly into Harry's chest sending him backwards onto the nearest wall. The man then forced his large frame through the doorway into the house.

CHAPTER 2

A MURDER OF CROWS

The three crows on the rooftop all spread their wings and flew as fast as they could toward the house. Steven and Barry went in through the open front door while Charlie smashed straight through the upstairs window, landing with a thud on the floor.

Samuel's music was so loud he didn't hear the bird smash through his bedroom window or the shotgun blast that had just killed his Dad. But as the crow turned into a fully-grown man behind him, he couldn't help but sense that something was wrong, spinning round on the spot.

For a second, he presumed it was his Dad. But as he noticed the man's rugged face and tattered clothes he began to panic, immediately reaching for a nearby baseball bat. As Samuel turned back around ready to swing his bat, he was surprised to find the man did not look scared and simply had one finger to his lips as if telling Samuel to be quiet. Samuel ripped his headphones off and discarded them to one side ready for a fight. That's when he heard the sound of a shotgun blast from downstairs.

Immediately presuming the worst Samuel charged at the man swinging the bat wildly. Charlie dodged the attacks with ease before grabbing the bat off him. As Samuel desperately looked around his messy room for a new weapon he was surprised as Charlie handed him the bat back.

"I'm here to help." Charlie whispered before putting a finger to his lips and tilting his head twice, motioning Samuel to follow him.

Charlie opened the door as quietly as he could and walked straight to the staircase, tip-toeing down a step at a time.

As they both descended, it was the perfect chance for Samuel to smack him on the back of the head but for some reason he trusted the man. As the pair reached the bottom of the stairs and turned the corner Samuel's face turned to horror. Beside the front door in a pool of blood was his dead father. Ten yards away in the middle of the sitting room floor was his dead mother.

"No!" Samuel cried, dropping his bat to the floor and running towards his Dad's corpse to try and wake him up.

As Samuel mourned aloud, Charlie ventured further into the house. He followed the open doors into the back garden where he saw the heavy-set man in the grey tracksuit looking through the bins. On the recently cut lawn lay the two dead bodies of Steven and Barry, their necks clearly snapped.

Charlie silently retreated back into the house as quickly as he could where Samuel was now attempting to wake up his mother.

"We have to go now." Charlie demanded pulling Samuel to his feet.

"Where's my sister?" Samuel asked, tears streaming down his face.

"I don't know but we really have to go." Charlie insisted.

But it was too late. The rotund man in the matching grey tracksuit was stood looking at the pair with a smile.

"I killed your two friends crow; do you fancy a go?" The man teased.

"No thank you, we are going now." Charlie answered, trying to pull Samuel out of the room. But Samuel wouldn't move.

"Did you just kill my parents? Samuel asked, a rage he had never felt before burning through him.

"Yes, and you're next." The large man answered with a smile.

"We can't take him on alone." Charlie announced trying to pull Samuel away.

"Then I will die trying." Samuel said before charging at the man who disappeared into thin-air just before Samuel got to him.

CHAPTER 3

THE BIRDCAGE

A man dressed in an all-blue suit knocked on a metal door with the side of his fist, the sound echoed up the length of the back lane he was stood in. The man that answered had piercing yellow eyes, like that of an owl.

"Wha' d'ya want?" The man shrieked looking up and down the back lane for others. It looked like he was alone.

"Who is it?" A woman's voice chirped from inside the building.

"I'm Greed, I'm here to see Mr Stork?" The blue-suited man announced with a smile. His stubbled jawline moving with his lips.

"Get lost." The man hooted before slamming the metal door shut.

"Who was that?" A woman perched on the edge of a nearby table asked, before she shoved a handful of seeds into her mouth.

Before they had a chance to realise what was happening Greed had walked through the solid metal door like it wasn't there and killed them both using a silenced gun. He then turned around and opened the door for his two scantily-dressed sisters. They walked together through a series of corridors before they arrived in what looked like a giant birdcage, full of every type of bird you could think of.

Ostriches, emus and cassowaries were walking around with babies and new-born animals tied to their necks. Smaller birds such as robins, sparrows and woodpeckers were feeding the children. In the centre of it all stood a six-foot Stork that was looking through a list of names.

"I want to speak to Mr Stork." Greed shouted over the squawking of birds, causing eventual silence in the room.

The giant Stork bird shook its white-feathered head and began walking down a series of steps to where Greed and his sisters were stood. Every step the bird took, he became a little more human. His spindly orange legs turned into bright orange trousers, his beak shrank back into a human shaped nose, his black-tipped wings became arms with hands on the end.

"How can I help you Greed?" Stork asked as his face fully humanised.

"Wow. You know my name, I'm impressed." Greed said with a proud grin.

"The Seven Deadly Sins are infamous, even in my line of work." Stork said with a little swish of his white feathered tail to complete the transformation.

"By the way if you were wondering, these two beautiful girls are Envy and Lust."

Stork glanced at the two girls in question. Envy was dressed in an emerald green corset with skimpy shorts and Chelsea boots to match. Her dark green hair sat in a bob cut with coloured tattoos covering every inch of her exposed skin, except from her face. She had hunting knives tightly gripped in each of her hands.

Lust was even more underdressed than her sister. Her bubble-gum pink shorts were even tighter and shorter than her sisters and her matching bustier crop-top was barely more than a bra. Her neon pink hair hung halfway down her back where she hid her pink clawed gloves.

"I wasn't wondering. Now I'm gonna ask you one more time before you become chicken food. What do you want?" Stork demanded.

"The Life Gem. If you hand it over now, I will let you and all of your feathered friends here live." Greed proposed.

There was a pause before the whole birdcage ruptured into a cackle of laughter, the noise was deafening.

"What time is it?" Greed asked his sisters while the laughter continued to echo throughout the cage.

"Who cares let's just do this?" Envy insisted.

Lust glanced at her Peppa Pig watch before answering.

"Three minutes past seven."

Oblivious to the tension inside the birdcage, an obese blonde woman walked into the room munching her way through a massive burger. She was dressed in a mustard-yellow t-shirt and jeans combo that was far too tight for her.

"Late again I see. Where's Wrath and Pride?" Greed asked impatiently.

"I dinno." Gluttony answered through a mouth-full of food.

"I've had enough of this, I have work to do. You all have ten seconds to leave." Stork demanded before beginning his countdown.

"Ten. Nine. Eight."

"Seven, six, two, one." Envy sped up.

"...Oh, I do hope I'm interrupting." A posh voice suddenly asked from the shadows.

A handsome man with jet black hair and stubble walked into the centre of the room. He wore a black suit and tie with shirt and shoes to match. He looked like he was dressed for a funeral.

Behind him was a man who looked angry with a passion. He had flame red-hair and was dressed in a matching red Sergio Tacchini tracksuit.

"You're both late." Greed snapped at the pair.

"Let's just get on with it shall we." Pride suggested before grabbing one of the nearby pigeons and snapping its neck.

CHAPTER 4

THE INVISIBLE MAN

Samuel stood rooted to the spot, trying to figure out what had just happened. The person who had just killed his parents had disappeared from right in-front of him. Out of nowhere, Samuel felt a blow to the face, so hard that it knocked him across the room. Charlie instinctively ran over and swung a punch at the spot his ally had just been struck. However, he hit nothing. As Samuel got back to his feet, Charlie was hit over the back of the head knocking him to the floor.

Samuel walked into the centre of the room with his fists clenched, ready for a fight. Three punches later, he was back on the floor with no idea where the invisible man even was. Charlie swung punches around the room hoping to make contact with the enemy. Each miss was answered with a laugh from somewhere else in the room. Eventually he was knocked to the floor again. Samuel got back to his feet and swung his fists wildly (desperately hoping for more luck than Charlie) but it was hopeless. Every swing missed its target, every miss was rewarded with a returning blow.

When the man finally appeared again, he was carrying his shotgun. He aimed it at Samuel and let out a smile.

"No!" Cried a little girls' voice from the kitchen.

Samuel looked up to see his sister running into the room, with a knife in her hand. She came to a stop as the man disappeared before her. Samuel climbed to his feet, desperate to hug his sister and keep her safe. But then she disappeared too. He followed her muffled cries as they faded from the house. As he lost the sound of her cries for help, he could do nothing but watch as a grey car screeched away down the street. Desperate to help her Samuel began hobbling down the street as quickly as his body would allow.

"Where you going?" Charlie struggled after him.

"To the police station." Samuel answered.

"It's no good. This is something they won't understand."

"Somebody just turned up, killed my parents and kidnapped my sister.

What else is there to understand?"
Samuel barked back, before continuing
his limp.

"He just killed two of my friends as
well." Charlie noted as he caught up with
him.

"Then all the more reason to go to
the police!" Sam shouted.

"Look. I'm not sure who that was
that we just fought. But I'm pretty sure I
know why he did what he just did."
Charlie informed.

"And why is that?" Samuel asked,
stopping in his tracks.

"Cos you're a Stork."

"He killed four people cos of my
surname? Bullshit." Samuel spat before
continuing his limp.

"It's not just a name though. We have powers." Charlie announced.

"What the hell are you going on about?" Samuel snapped at him.

"I can't show you here, follow me." Charlie announced, walking away from the growing crowds and nosy neighbours into a nearby back lane.

Samuel stood there looking pissed off, before reluctantly following Charlie into the back lane. As Samuel turned the corner, Charlie was gone. All he could see in the desolate-looking back lane was a single crow that seemed to be stood looking directly up at him.

Just as Samuel was about to ask where he had disappeared to, Charlie answered by turning from the crow back into a human being, back in the same rugged clothes he was in before.

"What. Are. You?" Samuel asked, still pissed off, but reasonably intrigued.

"A Stork, the same as you. We both come from a long line of Storks that can turn into birds."

"So, I can?"

"Yeah."

"Fine. Teach me how so I can go and get my sister back."

"I will, I promise. But we have to go to the Birdcage first. I have to tell my boss everything that has happened tonight." Charlie informed.

"Very well, lead the way." Samuel insisted.

CHAPTER 5

THE LIFE GEM

The floor of the birdcage was flooded with a mixture of blood and loose feathers. Pride and Envy walked between the corpses finishing off the flock of injured birds that had survived the fight. Their brother Greed had tight hold of a barely conscious Mr Stork.

"Where is the life gem?" He shouted once more, shaking the distraught-looking man like a ragdoll.

"I will never tell you." Mr Stork breathed, barely able to stay upright.

"An hour with Lust will change that." Greed promised. "She is going to…"

"...It is under the bird feeder." A voice interrupted from the back of the room.

The whole group looked over, on edge. They eased up when they noticed a teenager with bright white hair.

"Check it." Greed suggested to Gluttony.

Gluttony didn't look happy about having to move. A scowl from her brothers and sisters told her she didn't have a choice. She got up, walked over to the bird feeder and ripped it from the ground revealing a small hole containing a treasure chest. Mr Stork tried to get up and stop her but Greed slapped him to the floor.

Gluttony yanked the lock from the chest and opened it up to reveal a small glowing red triangle. She picked it out and threw it to Greed who caught it with a smile on his face.

"Why would you do that?" Mr Stork pleaded to the white-haired teenager who didn't acknowledge the question.

"Cos Jack Frost here isn't stupid. Times are changing and he wants to be on the right side of the stage when the curtain comes down, unlike you." Greed informed as he inspected the gem to make sure it was real.

The group glanced over as a large bloke in an all-grey tracksuit entered carrying a small girl.

"Here's fatty here." Pride teased.

"Better late than never tubs." Envy shouted, adding insult to injury with a giggle.

"Ignore them, did you finish the mission?" Greed asked.

"Parents dead. Two crows dead. Stole daughter in case son or other crow come back." Sloth informed proudly.

"Not bad thinking Sloth. Let's go, we are done here." Greed said marching towards the door. "Oh, one more thing, someone finish Mr Stork off." Greed finalised before leaving the Birdcage.

"Gladly." Envy said with an excited smile on her face.

"I will do it." Jack Frost suggested.

Envy looked disappointed and was about to fight Jack for it. In the end she decided she couldn't be bothered and shrugged her shoulders before she followed the rest of the group out of the birdcage. Jack stood there for a minute, contemplating what he was doing. He dragged his heels as he walked towards where Mr Stork was kneeling and stopped just in front of him. Stork tried to get up but had spent all of his energy trying to save the friends that lay dead around him.

"Please Jack. Don't." Mr Stork begged.

"I'm really sorry, this way is… easier." Jack said with a determination in his voice.

Jack forged a long icicle into his right hand. It looked sharp and cold.

"Please, I beg you." Stork pleaded.

Jack took a deep breath and shoved the icicle into the side of Stork's skull, killing him instantly.

CHAPTER 6

ENDANGERED SPECIES

The birdcage was disguised as a beautiful large house just outside of Newcastle city centre, so it didn't take Charlie and Samuel long to get there. As they approached the entrance in the back-lane Charlie's worry had turned to panic.

"That's not supposed to be open. Why is it open?" Charlie announced breaking into a run.

Charlie ran straight inside and dropped to the floor where two corpses lay, one man and one woman.

"Wait here. If I'm not back in five minutes, leave without me." Charlie announced, trying to hide the worry and suffering in his voice as he got up and marched further inside.

"I'm in this with you now, whatever happens." Samuel announced, following him with solidarity.

"And if this path leads to your death?" Charlie asked as they walked.

"Then so be it, as long as I can save my sister in the process."

The pair entered a room that had dozens of metal rings looped around its circumference. In front of them lay hundreds of dead birds floating in a soup of blood and feathers, it was a horrible sight. Samuel turned around and immediately vomited against the nearest wall while Charlie fell to his knees sobbing.

"I swear whoever did this will pay." Charlie eventually croaked before getting back to his feet.

Charlie walked to the centre of the room where an ordinary looking man lay dead on his back. His face still held the feeling of fear.

"Sorry you had to see this Sam, let's go." Charlie apologised.

Samuel wiped his mouth and was about to follow when he thought he heard what sounded like a baby crying.

"Wait. I think I heard something." Samuel insisted, pricking his ears.

"Probably outside. Come on, we have work to do."

Just as he was about to give in, he heard it again. This time clearer than the first. It was definitely a crying noise.

"I can hear a baby crying." Samuel announced.

Charlie stood still, listening intently. For thirty seconds there was nothing and then clear as day, he heard it too.

"Come out whoever you are. Whoever did this is gone." Charlie shouted into the room.

In the top-right corner of the room, a door Charlie never knew existed swung open. A couple of terrified looking owls emerged and flew down to where Sam and Charlie were standing. They hopped about sniffing and pecking the ground around the pair as if they didn't trust the two men that stood in front of them. Charlie pulled back the sleeve of his dishevelled looking hoodie to reveal a stork tattooed on his arm. It was evidence enough.

The two birds nodded at one another before they shifted into two nervous looking teenagers. One boy, one girl. Their wings stretching out into arms, their beaks shrinking down into a nose and a mouth.

"What happened here?" Charlie asked as soon as their transformation was complete.

"The Seven Deadly Sins, they came for the Life Gem." The girl informed.

"And did they get it?" Charlie asked.

"Yes. Every corpse you see died trying to protect it, including Stork." The boy added.

Charlie stood thinking for a moment.

"We have to presume they want the other gems, which means we have to

39

warn the other Festives. How many of us are left?"

"Not enough and we have some new-borns with us." The girl informed. "We hid them and ourselves during the battle."

"Fine, get them to the Aviary. The Sins got what they wanted so you should all be safe there for now. Me and Sam will warn the other Festives, we will start with Jack Frost."

The two teenagers went quiet and shifty again. It was obvious they had something to say but didn't know how.

"What?" Charlie encouraged.

"Jack. He was with them. It was him that killed Stork."

"What! Why would he do that?" Charlie asked through gritted teeth.

"What's happening?" Samuel asked, reminding Charlie of his presence.

"We will go see the other Seasonals, see if they're alive and if they can help us. Then we will round up the rest of the Festives." Charlie announced unconfidently.

CHAPTER 7

MR EASTER

9AM the following morning, inside of a pristine-looking chocolate egg factory, a six-foot tall white bunny dressed in a mismatched suit was walking along the factory floor with several small Fuzzy Lops hopping behind him. He stopped at a machine that was churning out Easter eggs and adjusted his yellow and green polka dot bow-tie.

"Now, can anyone tell me what secret ingredient we use in the chocolate that surrounds each and every egg that we make here?" He asked through his rabbity features as ordinarily as any human mouth could.

"Some childlike wonder and a sprinkle of joy." One of the little Fuzzy Lops announced rather proudly.

"Yes, but why?" Mr Easter encouraged before playing with his long bristly whiskers.

"So that we can bring laughter to every girl and boy." A different rabbit announced.

"Well done. Now what is…"

"Uncle! Uncle!" Two Eastern Cottontail rabbits interrupted as they sped along the factory floor towards him.

"What's wrong Ollie and Mollie?" Mr Easter asked as the pair tried to catch their breath.

"There's some people here. They barged into the factory looking for you." Ollie informed.

"Jack Frost is with them but they look scary." Mollie added.

"I'm sure it'll be fine. But start evacuating the little ones just in case." Mr Easter announced before he walked off leaving the group of rabbits behind.

Mr Easter walked through the factory with an intrigued smile on his face trying to guess who Jack's friends could be. He loved guessing games, but this one had him completely stumped. Eventually he found himself face to face with Jack and the strangers, yet he was still none the wiser as to who they were.

"Good morning Jack, what brings you here on this beautiful day and who are your wonderfully dressed friends?" Mr Easter asked, bowing to the group.

"Give us the Laughter Gem and nobody will get hurt." Jack Frost proposed.

The sound of Mr Easter's laughter echoed throughout the whole factory. Eventually it settled and he tutted before speaking.

"Not even an introduction before a threat Jack. Your manners have dripped away like an icicle in Summer." Mr Easter said with a disapproving shake of his head.

"Go get the gem Envy." Greed ordered.

"And who might you be little child?" Mr Easter asked as he noticed a little girl being held in place by a man in a grey tracksuit.

Mr Easter gave her a smile and a wave, but she was too scared to wave back.

"A Stork. But that is none of your concern." A woman dressed in a green corset and shorts asked as she removed two knives from her side and began walking toward Mr Easter.

"Interesting tattoos." He said as she neared him.

"Interesting tie. Not." Envy announced before she ran at him screaming.

Mr Easter didn't seem the least bit scared as Envy ran towards him. He waited patiently until she was about to strike, he leaned backwards onto his paws and kicked her across the length of the room using his hind legs. She hit one of the machines with such a force it knocked her clean out and stopped the machine chugging away.

Wrath (A red-haired man in a matching red tracksuit) ran towards the giant white rabbit with his metal baseball bat. He swung it as hard as he could but Mr Easter simply stepped out of the way. Several more wild-swings also missed their target, Mr Easter giggled every time he dodged an attack. He loved dodging games. Eventually he grew bored and planted a roundhouse kick on Wrath's face knocking him across the room near to his barely conscious sister.

"This is fun." Mr Easter said excitedly. "Who is next?"

Pride unsheathed his sword and stepped forward as arrogant as ever. He was as quick as Wrath was ferocious. But it wasn't enough and he found himself on the floor beside his siblings soon after.

"Let's show them how it's done girls." Greed said as he stepped forward with Gluttony and Lust.

Mr Easter waited for Greed to approach and then swung a kick at him, but he missed and landed on the floor with a hard thud. The giant white bunny looked surprised, dusted himself off, then tried again. Greed laughed as he hit the floor again, and again and again.

Mr Easter was so frustrated trying to land a blow on Greed, that he didn't notice Lust sneak up behind him and scratch the length of his back with her poisoned claws. He swung a paw towards her but it was grabbed mid-strike by Gluttony who picked him up and began squeezing him tightly in a hug. Mr Easter loved hugs, but this one was far too tight for his liking. He desperately tried to wiggle free as he began to feel his limbs getting crushed under her brute strength. As he struggled for air, he could see no way out of the squashing predicament.

Gluttony let go with a yelp as Ollie and Mollie bit into her legs. Easter dropped to the floor with relief before jumping up in the air and connecting an uppercut with Gluttony's face.

"I will hold them off, get the gem and get out of here." Mr Easter demanded to the two Eastern Cottontail rabbits that had saved him.

The two rabbits looked unsure of his orders and looked at each other for clarity.

"Go now… please." Mr Easter demanded, knowing they didn't have much time.

CHAPTER 8

A SEA VIEW

Charlie and Samuel had to get two trains and two buses just to get to the edge of North-East Scotland. With their boat trip not until 7AM the next morning, they were forced to stay the night in John O'Groats. The Seaview Hotel shone a brilliant white against the murky sky that had crept in over the course of the day. As they settled in for the night, the typical Scottish rain soon followed and lashed against every window of the hotel. To pass the time they both went for a drink in the hotel's bar.

"I'm not old enough." Samuel whispered as Charlie asked for two pints of Tennent's.

"It is to calm your nerves. Medicinal." Charlie whispered back as the barmaid sorted the change.

As they both sat down on black-seated stools in the corner of the room the barmaid disappeared and the pair were free to chat openly. As Samuel looked around the room, he noticed an array of trophies and photo's that spanned the length of the wooden bar. They reminded him of home and brought tears to his eyes.

"I need to save my sister, no matter what it takes." Samuel announced.

"I know, but we can't do it alone." Charlie said taking a sip of the lager.

"So, who are they? These other Festives." Samuel asked taking a swig of the lager and nearly choking on the contents.

Charlie couldn't help but laugh.

"That's horrible. Is that what all lager tastes like?" Samuel asked wiping the excess saliva and lager from around his mouth.

"Yeah, don't worry, you get used to it." Charlie said taking another gulp. "Right I'll fill you in. There are seven Festives and each of them is tasked with looking after a gem, as well as many other things."

"What do the Storks do?" Samuel asked, daring himself to go for another sip of lager and then realising that it wasn't too bad in smaller quantities.

"To deliver lost children and animals to their forever home." Charlie informed.

"And the other Festives?" Sam prompted.

"I'm not really sure to be honest. I know who they are, where they live, and the fact we all have a gem to protect."

"And we are on our way to see the Seasonals?" Samuel asked, growing more confident with his sips of lager. Every gulp made him feel more grown-up and less sober.

"Yes. Jack Frost is their leader. I've met him twice before and I don't believe there is a bad bone in his body." Charlie said solemnly.

"People can change." Samuel suggested.

"Festives are different to us. They have this aura of goodness about them. It's hard to explain but I feel like if Jack did kill Stork, it must have been for a good reason. Or somebody could be framing him. Argh, I just don't know yet."

The pair went quiet for a while, drinking their lager in content silence, while a flurry of rain tip-tapped in the background.

"Who are the other Festives then?" Samuel eventually asked.

"Stork and Jack Frost you now know about. Then there's Cupid, Sandman, Mr Easter, the Tooth Fairy and Santa Claus." Charlie recollected.

"You're winding me up?" Samuel said with a giggle.

"I'm not. Honest." Charlie maintained.

"No way. I don't believe you."

"You've seen people turn into animals, people disappear completely, but you don't believe in fairy tales?" Charlie mocked.

Samuel went quiet. Thinking about the disappearing man made him think of his parents and his sister again.

"I'm sorry." Charlie apologised realising his mistake.

"It's fine honestly. Anyway, I'm tired. I'm going to bed." Samuel declared before finishing his pint.

He pulled a disgusted face at the empty glass before marching off towards his room. Charlie didn't try and stop him. He knew he needed time to grieve.

CHAPTER 9

THE LAUGHTER GEM

Ollie and Mollie hopped through the factory as quick as their furry little legs could carry them. When they arrived at the golden egg statue, Jack Frost was already standing there holding the Laughter Gem from inside.

"That belongs to us Jack." Ollie declared.

"Yeah, you have your own gem." Mollie shouted, her dainty nose twitching with anger.

"I'm sorry. It belongs to them now." Jack said turning his back on the pair.

"Not if we have anything to do with it." Ollie shrieked charging towards Jack, Mollie hot on his heels.

They didn't get very far as Jack swivelled round and froze the very air that surrounded them both, suspending them in a block of solid ice. As Jack walked away, the siblings could do nothing but shout profanities in his direction.

It was a gruelling twenty-two minutes later when a colony of shadows came to their rescue, gnawing at the ice around them. Arctic hares, Cashmere Lops and Flemish Giant rabbits all worked together to free Ollie and Mollie.

"Quick. We have to save Easter." Ollie said shiveringly, once he was free.

"I'm sorry. We are too late." A six-foot tall pink bunny in a purple waistcoat announced.

"Aunty. What's wrong?" Mollie asked, leaping towards her.

"He. Is. Gone." Mrs Easter announced through a deluge of tears.

The whole group cuddled into a circle and sobbed together.

"I know this is a bad time but I have more bad news to inform you all." Mrs Easter eventually announced as the crying dissipated in the room.

Ollie and Mollie looked at each other with confusion, both wondering what bad news could be appropriate in the situation.

"I have just found out that Mr Stork is also dead and the Life Gem is also missing."

"They're going for them all, like the daemon Belphegor tried to do?" Ollie guessed aloud.

"It would seem so." Mrs Easter announced before wiping her face free of mascara.

"Do the other Festives know?" Mollie worried.

"I don't know, so it is our job to warn them." Mrs Easter confirmed.

"You're the leader now Aunty. Tell us what to do." Ollie announced.

"I have to get the rest of the warren safe so we are going to move everybody to the secret burrow. The rest of you are gonna warn the other Festives." Mrs Easter announced.

"Who is going where?" An Angora rabbit asked.

"Oreo, you're on Sandman. Hazel, get to Cupid, Thumper, warn the Tooth Fairy."

"What about us?" Ollie and Mollie protested at the same time.

"I want you both to get to the North Pole and warn Santa Claus. He will know what to do." Mrs Easter announced.

"Consider it done." Ollie announced before hugging his Aunt's left leg, Mollie hugging the right one.

"Good luck everyone." Mrs Easter shouted as she watched the group of rabbits all hop away in different directions.

CHAPTER 10

THE NORTH POLE

Santa Claus was sitting down at a small mahogany table in his office dressed in his usual red and white attire. He was merrily testing a series of fidget spinners when a robin with a beautiful red breast landed on his shoulder and tweeted something in his ear. Santa's prominent red cheeks flushed white in surprise, his normally jolly demeanour disappearing entirely from his face.

Santa pondered in silence for a moment before forcing himself to his feet. He whispered something in the bird's ear before stroking its little head and feeding it a single crumb from his pocket. The bird flew away as Santa marched out of the office into a candlelit room that was the size of a football pitch.

On either side of the room, there were rows of children-sized seats. Sat in each of them was a colourfully-dressed elf testing out a range of different toys. Some playing loudly with musical instruments and computer games. Some of them quietly playing with dominoes and decks of cards.

They all seemed oblivious to Santa's worry as he rushed through the factory. Once outside and out of sight he started frantically raking through his deep pockets.

Eventually he found what he was looking for, a Rubik's cube. He pulled it out and quickly solved it so all the colours were matching up before throwing it down onto the snow-covered floor. For a few seconds it did nothing, just lay there in the cold like an ordinary inanimate object. Santa gave it a confused look and a little nudge before it eventually sparked to life and began unwinding itself into a giant black square, opening a hole in the floor that looked like it led into complete darkness. He took a deep breath and jumped inside.

Santa landed on the floor of a small office with a thud. In the corner of the room was a desk where a teenage girl dressed for winter was sat counting names on a piece of paper. As Santa coughed to alert her of his arrival, she held a single finger up to declare she wasn't ready to be distracted. Eventually she finished counting and looked up to see who the guest was. Her face lit up as she saw Santa Claus.

"Uncle." She said getting up from the table and running over to hug him.

Her turquoise blue woollies melding with Santa's red and white ones.

"Anya. So good to see you. Sorry I haven't been for a while, I've been…" Santa started.

"…Busy. I know, me too." Anya finished in a mild Russian accent. "How is things?"

"Not good I'm afraid. Where's my brother?"

"Getting ready to go see Jack Frost, see if he can do anything about this crazy Russian weather we have been getting." Anya said pointing to the window where you could see it was snowing outside.

"I know it's Russia, but it is Summer for God's sake." Anya said with a giggle.

As she glanced back at her Uncle and saw his unusually stern face, she knew something was seriously wrong. She was about to question it when her father burst in through the front door bringing a draft of freezing cold air in with him.

Anya shuddered as her father stamped his feet in an attempt to rid the snow that was glued to his boots like white mud. He wiped the sleet from the shoulders of his azure blue coat and gave his hat a shake before he even bothered looking up.

"Hello brother. What brings you 'ere?" Jasper Klaus asked as he noticed the other presence in the room. He was similar to Santa in appearance. He had the same rosy cheeks and long beard, but all of Jasper's hair was grey rather than white, which made him look a lot younger than Santa.

"I need your help evacuating the North Pole." Santa declared with regret.

"Why the 'ell you wanna do something silly like that for?" Jasper squeaked with surprise.

CHAPTER 11

MAKING WAVES

Samuel and Charlie were visibly worried when a boat turned up for them early the next morning. It seemed to have more rust than it did paint. It looked over a century old.

"Please say this isn't our boat." Samuel whispered as the boat pulled into the jetty beside them. The word 'Nessie' was haphazardly painted onto its port-side.

"You the boys who wanna lift to Froome Island?" A deep voice yelled from the boat.

"Yes. Please." Charlie answered with a fake smile before climbing down the jetty and onto the boat.

Samuel reluctantly followed him as the man steadied the boat as best as he could. When they were on-board, he slowly turned her around and pulled away from the jetty.

"So, where ya from boys?" The man asked as the boat struggled to cut through the rough North Sea.

"South Shields." Sam answered quickly.

"Redcar." Charlie answered nonchalantly.

"Never heard o' either o' 'em I'm afraid..." The man admitted with a laugh.

They were both glad of this. The less they had to say about their home towns, the better. Neither wanted to remember their old lives for the time being, both for different reasons.

"...So, what brings you all the way up 'ere then?" The man asked with intrigue.

"Family." Charlie pretended loudly, trying to drown out any fabrication that Sam could murmur.

"On Froome Island. Didn't think any o' them 'ad any family." The captain squeaked with surprise.

"We are quite distant." Charlie lied.

"What you 'ere for then?" The captain turned his attention to Sam.

"Moral support." Sam guessed aloud.

"They must be distant if you need moral support to go and see a member o' ya own family." The captain joked.

Charlie and Sam both began to worry that their lies might get them into trouble. They were both relieved when the captain continued speaking, allowing them some respite from his interrogations.

"...Mind you. They are a weird bunch them up on Froome Island. No offence."

Charlie smiled, then realised perhaps he shouldn't be smiling seen as though the captain was mocking his fake family.

"What do you mean?" Sam encouraged.

"Well they aren't like normal people are they? Always keep themselves to themselves. Round 'ere we buy off each other, help each other out from time to time. But you never see any o' them, never mind get anything off 'em. They rarely even answer their own bloody door..." The captain ranted before suddenly altering his course as if he had forgotten where he was going. It turned out once you got the old captain talking, it was hard to get him to stop.

"...My neighbour Marjory once made a load of pies and left one on their doorstep for them. Three weeks later it was still there untouched. Bloody good waste o' food that was. And it's not just pies either. I've seen good quality marmalades; Dundee cake and the occasional scone go to waste. Nobody bothers now though..."

Sam and Charlie were trying their best not to laugh at the man's rant as he continued.

"And they have their lights on at all manners o' the day. I've gone past there at four in the morning a few times and their house is always lit up like an airport.

Gas and Lecky is expensive in these parts, you wouldn't have it on unnecessary like, unless you had money to burn o' course."

"And then there's the rumours." The captain added.

"What rumours?" Sam pressed.

"Well I heard on good authority that people like to get dressed up in funny costumes and visit all the time. Took a man dressed as Santa Claus there myself.

"When was this?" Charlie jumped in with a sudden interest.

"It was a good year ago now but still."

Sam and Charlie looked at each other in awe.

"To be honest with ya, I expected the two of you to be dressed up all funny this morning." The captain said with a laugh as the boat pulled into another jetty and the captain jumped ashore, tying up the boat with a couple of flimsy looking ropes.

Sam and Charlie struggled ashore as the boat rocked beneath them, both of them nearly falling into the cold-looking water a few times. They were both really glad to make it onto the jetty without a mishap.

"Well this is it, Froome Island. Sorry I've blabbered on. Once I start, I forget my place." The captain apologised.

"It's fine. Thank you very much. Your stories were great to hear. I will ring again if I need a lift back." Charlie said before giving the man a twenty-pound note. Double the price that was agreed.

"Are you sure? Thanks mate." The captain said before jumping back on-board and steering away before Charlie had a chance to answer.

CHAPTER 12

EVACUATION

Santa Claus pulled out a long candy cane from his pocket. The length of it should never have fit inside, but somehow it did. He pulled the stick apart to reveal a tiny set of ladders. He then extended the ladders until they almost stretched the length of the room. Santa then placed the ladders at the foot of the portal he arrived through and began climbing inside.

"Please hurry." He said before disappearing out of the other side.

"Some of the stuff he does never ceases to amaze me." Jasper said before following him through the hole. Anya laughed with wonder before doing the same.

Above them, lights were flashing all across the night sky and deafening booms that sounded like thunder could be heard somewhere in the distance.

"We must be quick. The dome will only keep them out for so long." Santa declared as Jasper and Anya joined his side.

"Who is 'them' by the way?" Jasper asked as they followed Santa inside a giant white building with painted red borders.

"The Seven Deadly Sins." Santa answered.

Inside the building, there were over a hundred elves running around like headless chickens, the panic clear on their diminutive faces. Santa took a deep breath and shouted at the top of his voice.

"CALM DOWN!" Santa ordered the elves, who stopped their hullabaloo immediately. Three of the elves quickly rushed over to see him while the rest of them stood around awkwardly awaiting orders.

As the room fell into silence, the sound of the repetitive booming in the background become more prominent, reminding Santa of his impending plight. As the three elves arrived at his feet, they only came up to his knees.

"What's happening Sir?" The tallest of the three asked.

"We need to evacuate the North Pole. There is a portal outside, Erika I need you and a couple of your fastest elves to get as many toys as you can through it before the enemy get here. When the dome falls, forget about what is left and just get everyone through the portal." Santa declared before raking through his deep pockets, eventually pulling out a red bauble.

"Once you are all on the other side. Stamp on this and it will close the portal." Santa added before handing the decoration over.

"Consider it done." Erika declared before running off and grabbing a couple of choice elves to help her.

"Jakob. I need you to help Jasper and Anya evacuate all of the animals." Santa declared before blindly examining his pockets again. Eventually he found his bunch of keys and handed them over. They were so heavy and numerous that the elf nearly fell under their weight. He was relieved when Jasper took them off him.

"Lead the way little one." Jasper encouraged, before him and his daughter followed the running elf.

"What do you need me to do boss?" The final elf at his feet asked.

"Get all of the elves outside and ready to leave, I'm gonna prep the reindeer." Santa declared before leaving the red and white building for a small barn outside.

Santa couldn't help but smile as he watched twenty-five oblivious-looking reindeer kicking straw at each other as they played together in the barn with Christmas music playing in the background. Rudolph's nose went bright red as he noticed Santa standing there watching them. He rushed over and cuddled into him, almost knocking Santa to the floor. All of the other reindeer noticed the new presence in the room and rushed over for the same attention.

"Alright. Alright. Calm down." Santa pleaded with a giggle as they swamped him in antlers and fur.

When he eventually got back to his feet, his smile faded into a serious looking face. One that the reindeer had rarely ever seen.

"Now. We need to quickly evacuate the elves. So, I need you to be serious for a while and all do as you're told." Santa ordered.

Rudolph snorted in disgust as the rest of the reindeer all stood up straight. Santa gave Rudolph a look that told him he was serious. Rudolph rolled his eyes before standing up straight and marching the other reindeer outside to a series of sleighs that were parked up like planes in an airport.

Santa strapped-up five reindeer to each sleigh with Blitzen, Donner, Prancer, Rudolph and Olive as the five lead-reindeer for each of the five sleighs. Santa then walked around giving them a carrot each, before whispering a location into their ears. As the panicking elves filled up the sleighs, the reindeer weren't the least bit worried about the obvious pandemonium.

When everyone was accounted for, the sleighs took off one-by-one and disappeared into the night sky leaving Santa alone in the snow.

CHAPTER 13

FROOME ISLAND

As soon as the captain and his boat were out of sight, Charlie broke into a sprint up the steep hill toward the brick building perched on a cliff top. Sam cautiously followed, apprehensive about what was about to happen. The three-story brick house loomed above them with a sense of abandonment. There were no lights and no signs of life. Charlie's deliberate loud knock on the wooden doorframe was not answered, neither was the doorbell that chimed an unimaginative 'ding-dong'. He pressed it again, but again there was no reply.

Charlie tried the door and was surprised to find that it swung open.

"Stay close." He ordered as he ventured deeper inside.

Sam followed with fear. He had already proven that he wasn't much of a fighter and the anger he had with him in the last bout had ran out. As he thought about his dead parents and missing sister it began to build again and in it, he found a slither of bravery.

The house was more like a show-home than somewhere that was lived in. There was no sign of anything that made a house a home. No photographs, no personal belongings, no flavour. There was also no sign of a struggle, or anything that could give Charlie hope that Jack Frost had been forced to join the Seven Deadly Sins.

"Hello." Charlie shouted with aspiration.

They waited patiently for a reply. There wasn't a sound, not even a mouse.

"Hello!" He yelled again, louder than the first.

Charlie's hope turned to desperation as he sprinted upstairs to look for a sign of life. From downstairs Sam could hear him raking through draws and cabinets, clashing and banging his way through every nook and cranny of the house. Then Sam heard something else. He couldn't make it out at first, over the rest of the noise. Then he heard it again. It sounded something like a cat purring. He followed it as best as he could until he was back outside.

Without the distraction of Charlie, Sam could make out the noise a little better. He decided it wasn't a cat at all, it was a fly or a swarm of flies. He cocked his ear to the wind and quickly followed it to the back of the house where he was greeted by a bright white light. The strength of it caused him to squint and stagger backwards. Sam felt a sense of nausea, followed by fear. As the light seemingly hovered slowly toward him, Sam slowly backed away from it.

As he retreated dangerously close to the cliff edge the light that was following him began to diminish, revealing itself to be a tiny little woman that was flying toward him with tiny little wings.

"Hello. I'm Aoife." The tiny woman said with a smile.

Sam nearly passed out with shock as the tiny creature spoke to him. This caused him to lose his balance and fall backwards. The creature instinctively grabbed Sam by the collar, but he was too heavy for her and he dragged the pair of them over the edge of the cliff and towards a plethora of serrated rocks perched below.

Aoife pulled and pulled with all her might but Sam was too heavy for her. His life flashed before his eyes as he descended, he saw his mother, then his father, his sister, then Charlie. Then something else entirely, a bird of all things. A giant white stork with spindly orange legs, and it was saying his name.

"Samuel fly." It said.

Out of fresh ideas and hope, Samuel put out his long gangly arms and began flapping them as quickly as he could. He watched with horror as they shrunk in size and changed in colour. Going from a long pink and fleshy arm into a brown feathered wing.

CHAPTER 14

THE GENEROSITY GEM

Santa Claus breathed a sigh of relief before running as fast as his heavy clothes would allow him to. He screeched to a halt beside a red and white sign that read 'North Pole' and began digging through the snow with his fingers. It didn't take him long to reach something that was covered in wrapping paper and a ribbon.

He prized it open messily, his hands shaking as they finally reached the contents inside, a box. He opened it to reveal a red triangular gem that glowed brightly. He temporarily put it in his mouth as he began raking through his pockets for something.

Eventually he found what he was looking for, a toy soldier. His hands shook violently as he struggled to balance it on the snowy ground. As soon as he managed to stand it up properly, he got up and ran back in the direction he had come from. He didn't get very far before the dome above him rattled like an old train and then disappeared.

As Santa picked up the pace he began panting like a heavy smoker. By the time he got back to the building he was running for, he was wheezing. Santa marched towards the back of the room where over one-hundred metal lockers stood in front of him. For a moment he tried to remember where he had put his yellow candle, but he had so much to remember lately that he was forgetting things.

"Santa." A voice called out from behind him, making him spin in anticipation.

Santa was surprised and disappointed to see that it was Erika the elf.

"What are you doing here? I told you to leave when the dome failed." Santa snapped in anger.

"I saw you come in here so I decided to stay behind and help you. Don't worry, I gave Hanne the bauble and told her to close the portal once they were through." Erika declared.

"I'm sorry, you're a good elf Erika." Santa said with a smile.

"I know." Erika replied with a cheesy grin.

Santa looked visibly upset, yet determined to finish the job.

"There's one more thing I need you to do Erika." Santa declared with a new sense of determination.

"Anything." Erika declared running towards him.

"I'm gonna turn my back and I need you to hide in one of these lockers."

"Why?" Erika questioned.

"Please just listen, we don't have long." Santa said searching through his left-hand pocket.

"Okay I will do it." Erika reaffirmed.

"This gem that I have is more important than both of us. I need you to take it and hide in one of these lockers with this candle." Santa said before handing over a triangular red gem and a small yellow candle that lit as Erika took hold of it."

"What are they?" Erika asked.

"The gem is an important artefact that cannot fall into enemy hands. When this candle burns down you will be transported to where the Sandman lives, he will help you. But you must stay inside the locker until then, no matter what happens out here." Santa instructed.

"But…"

"…Promise me Erika." Santa ordered.

"Okay I promise, just tell me what this is all about."

"I can't, you'll just have to trust me. Now do it." Santa ordered before turning his back on all of the lockers.

Erika seemed to take forever in her choosing, but eventually she picked the number '29'. She placed the red gem in her pocket, opened the locker with one hand and walked inside, closing it behind her. She would never have picked that number if she knew it contained a smelly old pair of socks inside. For a few seconds she debated changing her mind as the smell began to invade her nose. But a voice from outside the lockers told her it was already too late.

"Hello Santa, long time no see." A familiar voice said aloud.

"Jack Frost, I hear you've been a naughty boy." Santa said with disappointment.

"You heard correctly. My friends are here for the Generosity Gem. Hand it over and they will let you live." Jack offered.

"I honestly don't know where it is." Santa said confidently.

"He's lying!" An angry voice snapped back.

"He is incapable of lying. He must have passed it onto one of his cronies when we were trying to get inside." Jack informed.

"Like who?" A voice asked in frustration.

"Zwarte Piet or one of his brothers would be my guess." Jack answered with disappointment.

"Then we have no use for him then." A woman's voice declared.

"I suggest." Jack started. "We leave the Generosity Gem 'til last and go get the…"

Erika was really disappointed as the candle whipped her away from the conversation, replacing the smell of socks with a hint of smoke.

CHAPTER 15

FLYING HIGH

Sam was ecstatic as he soared through the sky. He would have laughed and smiled if his lips had not been replaced by a small black and yellow beak. He soared through the air above Froome Island testing his speed, agility, drag and thrust. Sam thought he was super-fast but the truth was he had no real comparison. As he watched little Aoife land beside the building on Froome Island he decided to test his own landing skills.

It was a decision he regretted immediately as he hit the floor with a thud, rolling over a bunch of times before slamming to a stop on the side of the house. As he achingly got up from the floor he realised he was no longer a bird but had gone back to being a full-sized human again, donning rags that half resembled the clothes he was previously wearing.

"What was I?" Sam asked Aoife enthusiastically.

"You were a bird. It was amazing!" Aoife squeaked excitedly.

"What type of bird I mean?" Sam pressed.

"I dinno. Some sort of kestrel or hawk. I don't know very much about bird types I'm afraid."

"Cool." Sam said blissfully.

Meanwhile inside the building, Charlie had looked everywhere he could think of for the Weather Gem, but there was no sign of it anywhere. When he finally gave in, he headed outside in search of Sam, where he was surprised to find him talking to a small speck of light. As he inspected it more closely, he realised inside the light was a small girl with a face that Charlie recognised.

"Aoife?" Charlie asked with bewilderment.

"Charlie?" Aoife asked, flying over as she saw who it was calling her name.

"You two know each other?" Sam asked with wonder.

"Yeah me and Charlie go way back." Aoife beamed as she landed on Charlie's shoulder, treating it like a bird might treat a branch.

"How are you by the way?" Aoife asked.

"Not good. You heard about the Birdcage?"

"No, what's happened?"

"We were attacked. Most of us have been killed, including Stork."

"Aw no that's awful, I'm so sorry to hear that, but I'm glad that you're okay at least. We had a feeling something was going down but this is way worse than we imagined."

"Aoife. I need to see the Tooth Fairy and warn the other Festives. Do you think that you could help me?" Charlie asked.

"You think the fairies are in danger?" Aoife worried.

"Yes. Can you please take us to the mansion?" Charlie pleaded.

"Yes. Huddle up you two. And close every orifice." Aoife instructed.

"What's an orifice?" Sam questioned.

"Just cover your mouth and nose and keep your eyes shut till we get there." Charlie advised. "The dust gets everywhere."

Sam and Charlie congregated beside Aoife who began to sprinkle them with a fine glowing dust before powdering herself.

As she sneezed the three of them disappeared.

CHAPTER 16

NIGHTMARE ON ELM CLOSE

Inside the bedroom of a terraced-house in Saltburn-by-the-Sea, Angela Diggory was reading her seven-year-old son Toby a bed-time story. Usually he would protest he was too old for such things but when she suggested it might stop the nightmares he had been having, he decided he would give it a go. She didn't even get to the second chapter of 'The Silver Chair' before he was snoring like a baby walrus. Angela got up quietly and delicately tip-toed to the door, turning off the light before she left the room.

As soon as the door closed behind her a figure floated through the window pane like it wasn't there. The figure was that of a man dressed like a Joker playing card with black and yellow stripes lining the length of his spindly body. He swam through the room as if gravity no longer existed, landing on the headboard right next to snoring Toby. The wasp lookalike then removed a tiny little mojo bag from his pocket and poured its contents onto the child's face. The mound of yellow sand seemed to glow as it began to find its way into the corners of the child's eyes.

"No more bad dreams for you." The Sandman whispered with a smile.

A creaking floorboard just outside the bedroom warned the weirdly-dressed man to expect sudden company. He looked around frantically for somewhere to hide and decided he had no other option than to fall backwards into the next-door neighbour's house. As he rolled through the thick wall and back onto his feet on the other side he found himself face to face with the ugliest of creatures, a Puggle.

The small dog snarled its disgust at the intruder and was about to bark its disdain, but before it had a chance Sandman touched its scrunched-up nose causing the dog to burst into an aggressive sneezing fit before yawning a big yawn, curling up into a ball and falling into a peaceful slumber.

With the dog temporarily suspended, Sandman decided he would explore the new surroundings he found himself in. It turned out he was in some sort of kitchen/living room mix and after a quick inspection he found the treasure of the house, their fridge. Despite it being taller than he was, it barely had any actual real food inside of it and the Sandman was forced to settle for two peanut-butter sandwiches which he wrapped up in clingfilm and placed in his pocket. He stole a Chalwa bar from the cupboard and headed straight for the wall in which he made his entrance.

Sandman took a deep breath and quickly popped his head into Toby's bedroom. He was pleased to find that only the boy was present in the room and he was still fast asleep. He climbed through the solid wall like it was branches of a tree and walked around to the boy's face. Sandman carefully blew around Toby's eyes to remove all the excess sand that still remained before running and jumping through the window without smashing the pane.

As Sandman floated through the air he looked for a high point in which he could enjoy his bait, eventually deciding on the rooftop of old Rushpool Hall. He ran through the air before screeching to a halt on the roof where he parked his bum and removed his battered lunch from his pocket. He munched on the crumpled peanut butter sandwich with joy before enjoying the squashed up Chalwa bar.

When he finally finished eating he removed a small yellow candle from his pocket and lit the end with a simple click. He took a deep breath and blew it out, disappearing with the flame.

CHAPTER 17

THE TOOTH FAIRY

On the edge of beautiful Borrowdale in the Lake District, Jack Frost and the Seven Deadly Sins were dropped off one-by-one by a daemon named Sitri.

"I hate him." Envy complained as soon as the daemon dropped off the last of them and disappeared.

"He is a means to an end." Pride reminded.

As the group walked along the road it forked off into two different directions. One route led up to a great mansion that sat dominating a hillside, the other snaked off towards the edge of a vast forest.

"This plan of yours better work Jack." Greed demanded.

"It will. Just go into the forest like I said and I will meet you there." Jack whined.

The Seven Deadly Sins shuffled away towards the vast woodland of trees while Jack climbed a steep road that led up to the mansion. As Frost got closer, he realised the place was lit up like an airport, despite it being the middle of the day. To an ordinary person it would look like the people of the house had simply left all of their lights on, but he knew the truth, it was lit up by fairy light.

As Jack arrived at the front door, he needed a minute to catch his breath. It was a much steeper walk than he remembered. He thumped the oil-rubbed bronze knocker against the door as loud as he could. It echoed through the mansion as the building fell into complete silence. He waited patiently for a reply but there was nothing.

He knocked again hoping his first knock simply wasn't loud enough. This time he thought he saw a ray of light shining through the peep hole. But again, the door wasn't answered. Jack knocked a third and final time. This time making sure it would be heard by using the fist of his hand to bang on the door afterwards. Jack waited for a minute then gave up hope.

As he turned around to walk back down the hill a voice called out to him from one of the windows of the mansion.

"Jack, is that you?" A familiar voice called out.

Jack span on heel to make sure the voice he heard was the voice he thought he recognised. His eyes lit up with relief as he saw the Tooth Fairy leaning out of one of the many windows of the mansion. She was wearing a long green sparkly dress that complimented her short green hair. Her wings fluttered behind her seamlessly as she flew down to Jack landing on the palm of his hand with ease. She ran up his arm and along his shoulder and kissed him on the cheek cuddling into his cold face with joy.

"I haven't seen you in, like... years. How are you?" The Tooth Fairy beamed.

"I'm okay. You gonna invite me in?" Jack pressed.

"Yeah of course." The Tooth Fairy said flying into the air and zapping the front door with her wooden wand.

The door seemed to fade into nothingness as the pair moved toward it.

"Sorry for the precautions, we've been hearing the most troubling of rumours." The Tooth Fairy announced as they entered the house.

As Jack looked around it was exactly as he remembered. An ordinary house full of ordinary things, that were getting used in the most peculiar of ways. Shoes were beds, sinks were swimming pools and a few of the fairies were using thimbles as hats.

The frolic of fairies watched with admiration as Jack and the Tooth Fairy made their way upstairs and along a corridor.

"Would you like a coffee Jack?" A fairy dressed in orange with ginger hair asked.

"Would you like some food Jack?" A fairy with a yellow dress and long blonde hair asked.

"Would you like..." One of the fairy men started.

"...Clear off you lot!" The Tooth Fairy demanded as they arrived at an office room. All of the fairies flew off in different directions leaving Jack and Tooth Fairy alone.

"So, what have you heard? The rumours." Jack encouraged as he began pacing the room.

"That Stork's gone AWOL, and the rest of you are looking for him. I presume that's why you have come to see me?" The Tooth Fairy asked while she checked a piece of paper that lay on the desk, turning her back to Jack.

"It's funny you've come here actually. I literally just sent Aoife looking for you." The Tooth Fairy admitted.

Sensing his opportunity Jack tip-toed towards her.

"I'm sorry Deanne." Jack announced, grabbing her tiny body and shoving an icicle to her temple. "Drop the wand."

"What are you doing Jack?" The Tooth Fairy asked as she let go of her wand and watched it fall to the floor with a quick rat-a-tat.

"Take me to the Belief Gem and nobody gets hurt." Jack ordered.

The Tooth Fairy yelped as she felt Jack's grip tighten around her miniscule waist.

"Okay, okay." The Tooth Fairy pleaded.

With a clap of her teeny hands, the pair off them disappeared from the mansion and found themselves in a vast forest.

CHAPTER 18

ENTER SANDMAN

When he opened his eyes again Sandman was no longer on the desolate rooftop of old Rushpool Hall. Instead he found himself in the mountains, stood next to a wooden bridge that led up to a great golden temple. Distracted by his own sense of happiness, he didn't even notice the tiny woman that was blocking his path until he was about to stand on her.

"Hey!" She yelled as he approached her petite frame.

"Hello there, child." He said, coming to an intriguing halt.

"I'm not a child thank you very much." Erika raged.

"No, I guess you're not. So, what are you?" Sandman asked curiously, checking out her small frame from front to back.

"An elf." Erika announced proudly.

"And why is an elf here?"

"I'm here to see Sandman. Santa Claus sent me." Erika announced trying her best to remain upbeat.

"Well I'm him. Pleased to meet you." The man said offering a hand.

"I'm Erika." She announced shaking three of his fingers gladly.

"Introductions sorted, now let me show you my home. Follow me." The man declared before hovering over the bridge, Erika jumping from wooden beam to wooden beam after him.

"What is it you need help with then? Night terrors. Erasing memories. Restlessness…" Sandman guessed.

As Erika reached the other side of the bridge, she had to catch her breath for a moment. The man noticed and stopped to wait for her.

"Truth is I don't really know what is happening, but it's something to do with this." Erika said removing the red triangular gem from her pocket and showing it to Sandman.

The man seemed shocked to see the gem glinting in his face, offended almost.

"Put it away, quickly, please." Sandman asked politely to which the elf promptly obliged.

Sandman thought for a moment before putting his index finger to the centre of the elf's head. Erika didn't know what he was doing so she just stood there in awkward silence while the Sandman did his thing. Whatever it was, it was over within a minute.

"What was that about?" Erika asked with an awkward giggle.

"I just read your mind." Sandman said matter-of-factly before marching toward the temple as if the conversation was over.

"Wait! You can't just bloody read somebodies mind without their permission. That's not..."

"...Don't worry. I won't tell anybody about the hair brush." The Sandman attempted to reassure.

Erika blushed with shock before running after him. But that wasn't her most pressing issue.

"Did you see what happened at the North Pole? With Santa Claus I mean." Erika asked as she caught him up at the entranceway to the temple.

"Yes."

"Do you think he's still alive?" Erika asked.

"Santa is smart I'll give him that. But your memory sounded like Jack Frost has sided with the Seven Deadly Sins."

"They're real?" Erika asked with fear.

"Yeah. So, in answer to your question, I honestly don't know if Santa is alive or not. But we are going to find out once I've moved the Dream Gem." Sandman announced before entering the great golden temple, Erika following him inside like a little lap dog.

CHAPTER 19

THE BELIEF GEM

The Tooth Fairy was surprised to find herself face to face with eight strangers. It didn't take her long to work out it was the Seven Deadly Sins, but the little girl alongside Sloth was a mystery to her.

"Well done Jack." Greed congratulated with a weak round of applause.

"Where is the gem?" Jack asked, reminding the Tooth Fairy of her predicament.

"Straight ahead, inside the tree of life. You're not working for these losers, are you?" The Tooth Fairy mocked.

"Once we have the gem, you are mine." Envy teased with a wink as Jack led her away.

"Shut up, you slut." The Tooth Fairy teased.

"Give her to me, she's dead." Envy raged trying to grab the fairy from Jack who stood his ground.

"Back off Envy. A deal is a deal." Jack ordered.

"That's fine. I don't mind killing the both of you." Envy said removing one of her knives from its sheath.

"Stop it Envy." Greed demanded. "Now!"

"But…"

"The Gem comes first Envy." Pride announced, grabbing Envy's hand and yanking her away.

"Fine." Envy moaned breaking free of Pride's hand.

Jack breathed a sigh of relief before following the directions of his hostage to the tree of life. As he stood face to face with it, he realised it wasn't what he expected it to be. He imagined a vast trunk that was as wide as a house and as tall as a windmill. In reality it was a small tree that looked like it had been planted just a year ago. He knew he was in the right place though, he could feel the power that was emanating from it.

"Where now?" Jack reiterated.

"Inside the roots. Just pull out the tree and you will see it straight away."

"Will it die?" Jack asked with worry.

"Do you care?" The Tooth Fairy said sarcastically.

"No." Jack lied.

Jack looked unconvinced with his mission. all of a sudden. It was as if he feared the repercussions of his next actions. The Tooth Fairy looked at him with surprise as Jack let go of her and got down on his hands and knees and began to pull the tree from the ground. It popped out like a weed revealing a small cluster of roots with a glowing red gem in its centre. Jack pulled the jewel from the root and attempted to replant the tree. But as it withered down into nothingness he looked down on it with regret.

"Sitri. We are ready for you." Pride shouted aloud, as if somebody was in the distance waiting for them. A man with jet black hair and gothic clothing appeared out of thin air, grabbed hold of Pride and disappeared again.

"It is time to teach you a lesson." Envy said running at the Tooth Fairy.

"No." Jack ordered, standing between the pair.

"May I?" Envy asked Greed, as Sitri grabbed Gluttony and skipped out of the forest.

"Just let her blow off some steam, we have the gem." Lust encouraged before she too disappeared with Sitri.

Greed simply shrugged his shoulders, not agreeing or disagreeing either way as Sitri skipped Wrath from the forest.

A smile lit up Envy's face as she kicked Jack out of the way and swung her knife towards the Tooth Fairy. The Tooth Fairy closed her eyes in anticipation. As Sitri disappeared with Sloth and Sophie Stork, Envy found herself frozen mid-strike. The Tooth Fairy opened her eyes to see that Jack had frozen Envy to the spot.

"Please, a deal is a deal." Jack pleaded to Greed.

"Very well." Greed consented as Envy disappeared out of sight with Sitri before the daemon returned for Greed leaving Jack and the Tooth Fairy alone in the forest.

"I'm really sorry Deanne. I have no choice." Jack apologised before Sitri returned for him and they both disappeared.

CHAPTER 20

STRANGERS IN THE SNOW

Ollie and Mollie dashed from building to building leaving footprints in the snow as they went. There was no sign of anyone or anything in the whole of the North Pole.

"Where do you suppose they went?" Ollie asked, scratching his long ears with his long feet.

"Beats me. But there are no dead bodies here, which means they probably all escaped." Mollie guessed as she tried to warm her nippy nose with her paw.

"Who are you?" A woman's voice asked from behind them.

The two startled rabbits turned in surprise to see a woman dressed in black jeans and boots with a dark red leather jacket. Her hair was white but her face looked young. Next to her was a man dressed in a red and purple jester gown who had half a white face and half a black face.

"Where did you two come from? We just searched the entire place. We are looking for Santa Claus." Ollie asked.

"You know Santa?" The woman asked hopefully.

"Yes." Mollie announced proudly. "Well. I've never met him personally. But him and my Uncle worked together."

"You're Ollie and Mollie, Easter's nephew and niece." The woman realised.

"Yeah we are. How do you know?" Ollie asked.

"Talking bunnies. Sort of gives it away." The woman admitted.

"Oh yeah." Mollie said covering her mouth as she realised that animals aren't supposed to talk.

"Well you know us, so who are you?" Ollie demanded, sniffing both their feet for clues.

"This is Zwarte Piet. I'm Nova, Santa's daughter. Pleased to..." The woman started before sensing something behind her.

"Somethings coming. Follow me." She said shooting the sky with her wand causing the calm ordinary day to slowly turn into a storm as the foursome retreated to the nearest barn.

Meanwhile in the middle of Russia, Jasper Claus was raking through a box looking for a red bauble. When he eventually found it, he handed it over to his daughter Anya.

"If I'm not back in ten minutes smash it." Jasper instructed.

"Please father, I should come with you. It's dangerous." Anya argued.

"That's exactly why you can't. I can't fight to my full potential if I'm worrying about you. Please, let me do this. You have other responsibilities right now." Jasper nodded toward the group of elves that were shivering by the fire in the corner of the room.

"Please be careful Dad." Anya said, hugging him tightly.

Jasper cuddled her back before removing a Rubik's cube from his pocket and attempting to solve it.

"My brother makes this look far easier than it actually is." Jasper quipped as he finally solved the cube and threw it against the nearest wall. As it settled to a stop the cube began unfolding into a portal that Jasper walked through with determination. As he ventured on, he realised that a blizzard was quickly surrounding him.

Jasper struggled to find his bearings in the snow storm that had suddenly enveloped him. Just as he was about to return home for his goggles, he noticed some half-covered footprints leading off to his left. He removed a handful of tinsel from his pocket and followed them into a building.

CHAPTER 21

THE MAN IN CHARGE

Jack Frost arrived in an underground temple that was clearly being kept up by a network of scaffolding. He didn't have a chance to react as he was slammed against the nearest wall by Wrath. Before he could even get back to his feet again, Pride grabbed him by the neck and lifted him up into the air choking him. Jack didn't dare fight back, he just closed his eyes expecting death to soon follow.

"Put him down." A voice demanded from the other side of the room.

Pride squeezed for a few more seconds before reluctantly letting go and dropping Jack to the floor.

"You think you can just do what you want and get away with it? You are our puppet remember!" Pride shouted in Jack's face before storming off.

"Actually, he is my puppet. Yet a puppet all the same. Aren't you Jack?" The male voice called out as it stood up from its darkened throne and walked toward the group.

"Yes Belphegor." Jack said through bated breath as the daemon approached him.

His body was thin and gangly and covered in scars. A long whippet tail followed his massive clawed feet along the room.

"Why is Envy an ice pop?" Belphegor mocked as he approached her. He closed his eyes and touched her frozen form, forcing the ice around her to quickly melt.

"She was gonna kill the Tooth Fairy." Jack petitioned.

Belphegor laughed hysterically.

"Attachment. It makes you beings weak." Belphegor noted as Envy finally thawed out. She immediately tried to go for Jack but Belphegor's hand stopped her in her tracks.

"Jack was an idiot, but we need him for now." Belphegor reasoned before he approached Jack and booted him across the length of the room.

As Jack hit one of the collapsed columns of the temple, he spurted out a mouthful of blood onto the floor. A smile lit up Envy's wet face.

Belphegor leaned over and whispered into Envy's ear.

"We can kill him when we get all the gems, but for now he is your best friend."

Envy giggled with excitement as Belphegor approached Jack and yanked him back to his feet.

"Leave us." Belphegor demanded before waiting patiently for the room to clear.

"I hope you aren't forgetting that I have your three sisters locked up, ready to torture or kill, if you don't follow my orders." Belphegor reminded.

"Two." Jack corrected.

"How two?" Belphegor asked, clearly confused.

"You said if I get half the gems you would release one of them."

"Yes I did. But I only count three Jack." Belphegor noted, pointing to a door that had three red gems attached to its surface.

"I count four." Jack said, producing the Belief Gem from his pocket.

"Ah, you did get it. Not as stupid as you make out after all." Belphegor smiled, snatching the gem from his hand and walking for the door with the three red gems attached to it.

"So, you'll release one of my sisters?" Jack pressed.

Belphegor ignored his words while he placed the gem inside a little slot. It glowed bright red with the others as it confirmed its match within the door.

"Yes. A deal is a deal. Any preference?" Belphegor beamed.

"Jennifer." Jack tried.

"Sitri!" Belphegor shouted into the room.

Within seconds the daemon Sitri arrived and stood to attention.

"Yes sir."

"Release one of the girls, but not Jennifer."

"But…" Jack cut in.

"DON'T EVER QUESTION MY KINDNESS AGAIN!" Belphegor boomed at the top of his voice.

"Sorry." Jack said, hanging his head.

"Sorry, what?" Belphegor rallied.

"Sorry master."

"Good, now if you go get me the gem from Sandman, I'll release her next." Belphegor promised.

CHAPTER 22

THE MANSION

Samuel and Charlie struggled to march up the hill that led to the faeries' mansion. By the time they reached its doors they were both out of breath and needed a minute to compose themselves.

"Why didn't you both just fly up?" Aoife asked with laughter.

"Cos he can't…" Charlie began before he finally realised Samuel's clothes were a little more beaten than before. "…Wait, did you?"

Samuel simply nodded with a proud smile.

"Oh wow, that is amazing. What are you then?" Charlie beamed, embracing Samuel with a hug.

"Erm. Some sort of hawk... I think." Samuel shrugged.

"Cool. I will have to teach you a few things later, but for now let's get this sorted." Charlie indicated to Aoife.

Aoife pulled out a small wooden wand and cast a spell on the door of the mansion.

"Follow me." She said, flying full-speed at the door.

Samuel was worried she was going to hit it with a bang. He was pleasantly surprised as the entire frame disappeared before she reached it. The pair of them followed her through the missing door with wonder.

The mansion looked like a strange mix of outdoors and indoors with plants growing from all sorts of nooks and crannies. Japanese Sago blooming from old kettles. Ivy growing over the top of three-piece sofas and Rainbow orchids sprouting from open drawers. But the beautiful decoration seemed to sink into the background as the trio noticed the chaos of fairies flying around bumping into each other.

Aoife grabbed one of them and give them a good shake.

"What the hell is going on? Why are you all flying 'round like bleeding idiots?" Aoife questioned.

"Jack Frost has kidnapped the Tooth Fairy. Whatever will we do?" The fairy pleaded.

Aoife, Samuel and Charlie were shocked into silence. As determined as the three of them were, they didn't have a plan or a clue about what to do next.

"Everybody calm down! I'm fine." An upbeat voice declared to the full mansion.

As if by magick the uproar ceased and everyone went back to their normal business of casually lazying around.

"Thank God. What happened?" Aoife asked, zipping over to give her boss a hug.

"Jack was after the Belief Gem. Once he got it, he let me go."

"That's just what we came to warn you about." Charlie announced disappointedly.

"Hi Charlie." The Tooth Fairy said before landing on his shoulder and giving him a hug. "Who is your friend?"

"Deanne this is Samuel Stork. Samuel this is Deanne, the Tooth Fairy."

"Another Stork. Pleased to meet you! How's the family by the way?" The Tooth Fairy asked.

"Deanne. We need to talk. We will be back in a few minutes Sam." Charlie announced before leading her away.

"While they are catching up can I pretty please show you my tooth collection?" Aoife asked, clapping her little hands together excitedly.

"Yeah sure." Samuel said with a smile before she led him off to one of the many rooms of the mansion.

CHAPTER 23

PEAS IN A POD

Jillian Sprout was a wisp of a woman at the best of times. But as a prisoner she had lost weight, making her already oversized musty coat look more like a tent on her. Her hair, that hung as brown knotted curls, ran down to her waist and her bottoms were covered in moss. She was busy watering the nettles in her cell when a voice interrupted her.

"It's your lucky day Spring." Sitri declared through gritted teeth as he opened the door to Jillian's cell.

"Oh really, how come?" She asked sarcastically, continuing to water the parched weeds.

"Cos you're being released." Sitri scowled.

"What have you done with my sisters? And Where's Jack?" She questioned as she was dragged from the cell by two daemons.

A strike to the face dazed her and she fell to the floor with a thud before a kick to the abdomen caused her to wince in pain. She looked across to the solid stone wall in front of her hoping for reprieve and praying for rescue.

Then out of nowhere the wall completely vanished. Replacing the stone-grey rampart with a calming view of the sea. Waters she recognised, smells she remembered. She glanced around, looking for where the next blow might come from, but there wasn't one. She was alone now. Jillian painfully got up and viewed her new settings hopefully, then she realised where she was.

She was home, back on Froome Island.

Meanwhile, back at the underground temple, the Seven Deadly Sins were patiently waiting for their next mission.

"Why are you still walking around with that stupid kid Sloth. Just eat her already." Envy teased, which put the other Sins into a rupture of laughter.

"Because she is a good bargaining chip." Sloth mumbled quietly.

"I bet you'd prefer she was a chocolate chip." Pride joked, which incurred an even bigger roar of laughter.

"Oh look, it seems the master let him live after all." Pride moaned as Jack Frost walked into the room.

"I hope you're a better fighter than you are a comedian, cos we are about to go after the Sandman." Jack quipped.

"We managed to put down the legendary Santa Claus with a simple bleed spell. The Sandman will be a piece of cake." Pride boasted.

"Sorry, but it's not that type of cake Sloth." Envy teased causing the group to laugh at him again.

"I don't know what you've heard, but Sandman is the toughest Festive of the lot. He can fly quicker than Stork, he's a better fighter than the Easter Bunny and his knowledge of magick rivals Santa and the Tooth Fairy. I'm just hoping he hasn't heard that I've switched sides yet." Jack declared, which silenced the group.

As Sitri walked into the room cleaning his hands with some antibacterial wipes, the group knew it was time for their next mission.

CHAPTER 24

ENEMIES/FRIENDS

Once they were both inside the golden temple, Sandman turned and blew the big heavy doors shut before ushering a wave of yellow sand to cover all of the windows of the room, as Erika watched with wonder. She had seen Santa do some awesome magick tricks in the past, but she had never seen him do that.

The inside of the temple was a brilliant shiny gold just like its façade. As Erika looked around, she realised she was in a circular room that had two men and two women, all praying to a statue that looked like it was made from sand. They were dressed in yellow monk like robes and wore long dreamcatchers around their necks. As they finished praying, they got to their feet and noticed Erika for the first time.

"Why have you sealed the door and windows and who is this child master?" One of the women asked, inspecting Erika's body with intrigue.

"I'm not a fricking child." Erika snapped.

"It's something called an elf. Keep it safe while I go get the Dream Gem." Sandman ordered before disappearing up a series of steps.

Sandman stopped in what appeared to be a bedroom and started raking around in all of the drawers and cabinets of the room.

"Can I help you?" A voice asked from behind him.

Sandman swung around to see who it was.

"Jack Frost. Thank God. I'm looking for the Dream Gem, but I can't remember for the life of me where I put it. Could you do me a favour and check them drawers over there please."

"Certainly." Jack said with a grin before searching in the corner of the room.

As Jack foraged through everywhere small enough to fit a gem, Sandman floated up to him silently and touched the back of his head. The Sandman flicked through his memories like a book, starting with the most recent pages and working back to when Jack was a small boy joyfully playing with his three little sisters.

"Ger' off im." A woman's voice yelled before Sandman felt a sharp pain in his stomach. He looked down to see the handle of a knife protruding from his belly. Sandman let go of Jack as he pulled the knife out and inspected the blade that was covered in his golden blood.

"Thanks Envy." Jack said freezing Sandman's feet together causing him to fall to the floor with an awkward thud.

It was as he lay there bleeding out onto the floor that Sandman noticed the crashing and banging noises that were happening downstairs.

"The gem is here somewhere Envy, help me look for it." Jack said, quickly raiding the cabinets again.

"Looking for this?" Sandman asked.

As the pair turned around, they were surprised to see the Sandman was floating in the air holding the Dream Gem in the palm of his hand. His icy restraints and his stab wound had completely vanished.

"You can have your knife back." Sandman said throwing it into Envy's leg who fell backwards with a scream. As Jack tried to counter with an ice spell, he found himself knocked over by a wave of yellow sand that pinned him to the nearest wall. Before he knew it, he was unable to move with the weight of the mountain of sand that covered him.

"Bye." Sandman waved before leaving the room and heading downstairs where he was shocked to see two of his colleague's dead on the floor. The other two were being held as hostages alongside Erika.

"Give us the Dream Gem and we'll give you your friends back." Wrath suggested as he tightened the grip of his baseball bat around one of the captives.

Sandman floated down to the floor and began to pace the room as if he was deep in thought.

"The gem or they die." Pride demanded, bringing his sword up to the neck of the man he held captive.

"Kill them, I dare you." Sandman eventually instructed with a smile.

CHAPTER 25

BLOOD TIES

Ollie, Mollie, Zwarte and Nova found themselves inside a big empty factory about the size of a football pitch. The candlelit room contained dozens of discarded toys and games.

"Wait. I'm confused. I thought we looked everywhere but I've never seen this room before." Ollie said as he picked up a pack of cards and looked through them.

"Yeah we definitely didn't come in here." Mollie confirmed.

"It's the main factory. You can only see it or get inside if you know it's here. Clever for keeping the public out but not if a friend turns against you." Zwarte explained.

As she looked around for clues, Nova thought she spotted something and suddenly rushed toward the back of the room near a line of lockers. The others instinctively followed.

"What is it Nova?" Zwarte asked as Nova leaned over what looked like a big puddle.

"Blood, and lots of it. Whoever this belongs to can't possibly have survived." Nova said getting up from the puddle and marching over to the rabbits.

"You have a good sense of smell right?" Nova asked hopefully.

"Only the best, why?" Mollie informed.

"That puddle of blood, can you give it a sniff and tell me what it smells like."

"Erghhh. No. Sorry I'm doing that." Mollie protested, trying her best not to be sick.

"I'll do it." Ollie said, before bouncing over to the pool of thick red blood. He carefully pushed his nose as close as he could without touching it and took a deep whiff. He began coughing on its sickly-sweet smell.

"Well?" Nova urged.

"Cinnamon. It smells like cinnamon." Ollie answered to the best of his knowledge.

"Now come over here." Nova voiced, before removing a small knife from her red leather jacket. "Smell my blood, does it smell the same?"

Nova slowly cut the palm of her hand with the knife. Making sure to get a decent bleed but not too deep. She winced as she did it. Nova clinched her hand to generate a pool of claret and then held it out for the rabbit. Ollie leaned in and inhaled deeply.

"Cinnamon." He declared, dropping his head with sadness.

"So, it's definitely Santa's blood?" A voice asked from behind the group.

Nova instinctively pulled out her wand but found her hands suddenly wrapped up in tinsel, causing her to drop it to the floor. Zwarte made a run for her wand, he got three steps before his feet were tied up in the same coloured tinsel and he hit the floor with a whump. The rabbits screamed and charged at the mystery figure who laughed at their pathetic stature.

His smile disappeared as the infinitesimal mammals turned into human-sized rabbits and rugby-tackled him to the floor. As he finally squirmed free of their fury grips, he found himself face to face with Nova's wand.

"Hello Uncle." She said with a smile.

CHAPTER 26

THE DREAM GEM

Everyone in the room was shocked by Sandman's declaration. Pride's bluff had been called and it left him lost for words for once.

"You are willing to throw away your friends' lives at the drop of a hat like that?" Greed asked.

"It won't be for nothing of course. You kill them. I have nothing to worry about anymore and kill all of you. Sounds like fun to me." Sandman suggested.

"You think you can kill all seven of us." Greed said confidently before realising he was two teammates down. "Wait, where's Envy and Sloth."

"Sloth disappeared with the kid when the fighting started and Envy went after Jack." Lust informed, tightening her grip on the elf she held captive.

"Look. All we want is that stupid gem in exchange for your friends. It seems like a fair deal to me." Greed suggested.

"Erika, can you hear me." A voice asked from inside her own head.

"Yes." She said aloud.

"Do you still have the gem Santa gave you." The voice asked her.

"Yes." Erika said with a smile, finally realising it was Sandman.

"Why do you keep saying yes for?" Lust questioned, looking down at the elf. "Come to think of it, why is there an elf here?"

"Fine." Sandman shouted into the room. "I will give you the gem if you release my three friends first."

"Wait, Greed. Something else is going on here." Lust cut in.

"Not now Lust. Release the prisoners everyone." Greed demanded.

Pride and Wrath reluctantly let go of the man and the woman in the yellow robes. However, Lust kept tight hold of Erika.

"Greed listen to me." Lust tried.

"Let her go Lust. I won't tell you again." Greed demanded as he approached the Sandman.

"Here is the gem. We are leaving together…" Sandman declared, handing the gem over to Greed. "…But if any of you try anything, I will kill you first."

"Very well." Greed agreed.

Lust scorned in silence as Sandman and his three friends walked out of the temple. She kept her mouth shut until they were gone.

"Greed I think that elf may have had Santa's gem. Why else would Sandman just suddenly change his mind like that."

"It doesn't matter. We have the gem we come for." Greed said before walking into the corner and grabbing Sloth by the neck and throwing him across the room where he became visible again.

Greed approached him again, ready to continue his punishment but he was stopped by a little girl standing in his way.

"Please don't hurt him. He was just protecting me." Sophie Stork protested.

"He killed your parents and you would still protect him." Greed mocked.

"He apologised and I forgive him. Everybody makes mistakes." Sophie reasoned.

Greed got down on his hands and knees so that he was roughly the same height as Sophie.

"You are our trump card for later. That is the only reason you are still alive. We are monsters. Don't think any different." Greed proclaimed in the most condescending tone possible, before disappearing upstairs to look for Jack and Envy.

CHAPTER 27

PLAN OF ACTION

While Charlie and the Tooth Fairy caught up, Samuel looked through Aoife's tooth collection. While he expected this to be a gory and excruciatingly boring experience, it was actually quite interesting. Hippopotamus canines, African elephant molars and warthog incisors were the crowns of her collection. Nevertheless, he was glad when a fairy named Niamh told them to meet Charlie and the Tooth Fairy in the garden. Once outside, they got straight to business.

"Right Sam. I have some news to tell you." Charlie began.

"Okay. What?" Sam pushed with worry.

"We think your sister is still alive." The Tooth Fairy declared.

Samuel nearly broke into tears. If he was alone he would have, but he tried his best to compose himself in front of the others.

"How do you know?" Sam pressed.

"When Jack and the Seven Deadly Sins took the Belief Gem from Deanne, she noticed Sloth was walking about with a little kid. She sounds identical to Sophie." Charlie informed.

"Good. When are we gonna try and get her back then?" Samuel asked, half-expecting more excuses and put-offs.

"Soon." Charlie assured. "The Seven Deadly Sins have already stolen the Stork Gem and the Tooth Fairy Gem. We are now presuming they already have most of the others, if not all of them."

"It is our job to try and get them back." Deanne announced.

"Who is gonna look after the mansion while you're away?" Aoife asked apprehensively.

"Your brother Cian." The Tooth Fairy declared.

"But I should be running the place. It's what you've trained me up for. I've been shadowing you for years…" Aoife protested.

"…You're coming with us Aoife." Deanne revealed.

"I know but I've been… Wait. What? Really?" Aoife realised happily.

"Yes."

"Oh good." Aoife clapped excitedly. "What's the plan then?"

"So, we are hoping they still have gems to collect, which leaves the Ianua Temple unguarded. If it's still intact that is." Charlie informed.

"Sorry, I'm new to all this. But let's see if I got this right." Sam announced. "There are seven Festives protecting seven gems. We are gonna try to get the gems they have already collected, while they are out getting the other gems?"

"Exactly." Charlie confirmed.

"But how does my sister come into it? You want the Sins out the way when we get to this temple, but my sister will probably be with them."

"Cos Aoife is going to disappear with the gems when we get them. But we are gonna stay back to try and get your sister." Charlie announced.

"Okay, when do we go?" Samuel asked, taking a deep breath.

"Tomorrow. But first, Deanne and Aoife are gonna practice some spells while me and you do some flying lessons." Charlie announced excitedly.

CHAPTER 28

BRANCHING OFF

Jack Frost, Sophie Stork and the Seven Deadly Sins were all relieved as they arrived back in Ianua temple. The battle with Sandman could have gone much better. It could also have gone much worse. Envy hobbled behind the rest of them grateful to be alive.

"Well. Do you have it?" Belphegor asked impatiently from his throne.

"Yes Master." Greed announced proudly, offering it to Belphegor who plucked it from his hand and walked over to the door.

He placed the gem in its own little aperture causing all five of the gems to glow bright red.

"Two to go." Belphegor announced proudly. "My daemons have tracked Cupid to Paris. Once we have an exact location you can go and get his gem. Then we will use the child to trade for the last one."

"My sister." Jack interjected.

"I will have her released shortly, don't worry. I have a potion that will help you with your leg Envy. The rest of you, go have something to eat and relax for a change. You have all done well." Belphegor rewarded.

*****

Jennifer Kindle was clicking her fingers in boredom. Every time they clicked together a little flame emanated from her fingers and lit up the small cell that she was stuck inside of. Her singed metal armour (that was far too big for her) glinted the reflection of the flame and her short black hair before she blew it out and then clicked again.

"Hands against the wall Summer." A voice called from outside of her cell.

Jennifer obliged quickly. She didn't want to miss out on the slop for being too slow again.

"Don't you dare move." Sitri scowled as he entered her cell.

"I won't." Jennifer promised.

"Legs further back." Sitri demanded.

Jennifer shifted her feet backwards so she was fully leaning against the cold brick wall. Suddenly she felt herself falling through the air as the wall disappeared. It was a fifteen-foot drop and there was nothing she could do about it. She was relieved as something or someone caught her, softening her fall.

*****

"But it looks horrible." Sophie Stork protested.

"I know, but you have to eat something." Sloth argued.

"I want turkey dinosaurs." Sophie complained.

"Will you shut that child up Sloth!" Envy spat before painfully adjusting in her seat. The bandage covering her wound turning carmine red as she moved.

"Please eat. I will be back in a minute." Sloth whispered.

"Where are you going? You can't leave me." Sophie panicked, grabbing his hand.

"Don't worry. I'm just talking to Jack." Sloth reassured before breaking free of her grip and approaching Jack Frost, who was sitting alone at the other end of the room.

"Jack, can I have a word please." Sloth started.

"What do you want Sloth?"

"Look. I know you might not believe me but I don't want to be bad, I never have. I'm just scared what the other Sins might do to me. I just want a quiet slow life that's all."

"Why are you telling me this?" Jack questioned.

"Cos I need your help getting out of here with Sophie." Sloth explained.

"You want to escape?"

"Yes. I know you're a good guy and why you're doing what you're doing. But you have to help us get away from them..." Sloth whispered glancing over to his siblings. "...Please."

Jack looked awkward. Like he didn't know what to do or say.

"I will try..." Jack agreed. "...You will have to wait for the right moment though."

"Fine. When will that be? How will I know?" Sloth grilled.

"Tell you what. I will call you fatty from now on. If I ever call you your true name again. That's your chance to leave with Sophie. Do you understand?" Jack instructed slowly.

"Yes. Thank you, Jack."

"And don't tell a soul. Not even Sophie." Jack ordered.

Sloth simply nodded then rushed back over to his table where Sophie was forcing down her dinner.

"What you grinning about chubby?" Pride teased from the corner of the room.

"The food." Sloth lied before tucking back into his slop.

CHAPTER 29

A BRIEF REUNION

Nova put her wand away and helped her Uncle back to his feet.

"Sorry about the tinsel." Jasper apologised.

"We are sorry we attacked you." Ollie and Mollie squeaked together.

"Mollie, you're big!" Ollie realised.

"Wow. So are you." Mollie informed.

"How did we?" Ollie asked pointing at their new statures.

"No idea." Mollie admitted.

"Can we talk about sizes later. I have to get back to the portal before

Anya closes it." Jasper declared before rushing off into the storm outside.

"Oh, sorry about the weather." Nova shouted through the miserable storm.

As Jasper rushed through the blizzard, Nova pointed her wand into the sky and started twitching it about as if she was trying to fit it into an invisible lock. Eventually it clicked into position and the storm began to dissipate. As Ollie, Mollie, Zwarte and Nova began trudging through the snow after Jasper, he managed to make it to the portal just in time.

"Wait!" Jasper yelled through to Anya who was about to smash the bauble.

Anya breathed a sigh of relief as she saw her smiling Uncle on the other side of the portal. She put the bauble down and rushed through to greet him.

"I started panicking when I saw the storm build as you went through." Anya admitted.

"Don't worry, I'm fine." Jasper relieved.

"Hello cousin. Long time, no see." A woman shouted over to Anya.

Her eyes lit up as soon as she noticed who it was.

"Nova." Anya screeched, dashing through the snow.

Anya hugged her cousin before hugging Zwarte Piet.

"Haven't seen you for a while Zwarte." Anya noted. "And who are these giant bunnies?"

"We are nephew and niece of the Easter Bunny." Ollie announced proudly.

"Awesome. How is he? Haven't seen him since I was five or so." Anya asked.

"Jack Frost and the Seven Deadly Sins killed him." Mollie announced as tears rolled down her face.

"What, when?" Jasper asked in shock.

"There's something else." Nova interrupted, hanging her head. "There is a pool of blood in the factory that belongs to Dad."

"How bad was it by the way? Do you think he could still be alive?" Jasper interrogated.

"If I had to guess, I'd say all eight of them have cast the Bleeding Madness spell on him at the same time. Dad's a genius but there is no way even he can survive losing that much blood." Nova admitted, wiping away the tears that rolled down her face.

"You never know. My brother is a miracle worker after all." Jasper tried.

"Your brother is dead. Deal with it..." Nova snapped before attempting to compose herself with a series of long deep breaths.

"...Zwarte stay with these. It's not safe for you to come with me anymore." Nova announced, removing her wand and drawing a circle in the snow.

"Wait. Where are you...?" Jasper started, but it was too late Nova had already disappeared into thin air.

CHAPTER 30

CUPID

Cupid stood out like a sore thumb in his fuschia pink suit and salmon pink shirt. His bleach blonde hair was styled as a fade cut, short on the sides, long on top. His dark sunglasses reflected the neon beams that were flashing throughout the nightclub. Cupid preferred his own company, sat at the bar drinking cheap vodka and coke.

"Puis-je vous offrir un verre.?" A beautiful dark-skinned woman in a long red dress asked, sitting next to him at the bar.

"Sorry. English." Cupid shouted over the David Guetta tune that was blasting throughout the nightclub.

"I said, can I buy you a drink?" The woman reiterated in a French accent.

"Yeah sure. Vodka and coke." Cupid said with a smile.

"Vodka illimitée et coca dans le stand deux, s'il vous plaît." The woman asked the barmaid before getting up.

"Come on you. We are going to…"

"…Cabin two." Cupid said with a smile.

The woman gave him a look of confusion.

"I speak French, I just prefer English is all." Cupid said as they marched off to booth two together.

"Clearly not that well." The woman said with a giggle as they got comfy in the secluded zone and shut the curtains. The material seemed to block out the music just enough to make the conversation bearable.

"I'm Gabrielle. You are?"

Cupid paused to think of a name.

"Don't tell me you've forgotten your own name?" Gabrielle asked before laughing at him.

"Look." Gabrielle assured. "I don't care if you have a partner. I don't care if you wanna lie to my face. I'm just here to have a good time. All I ask is that you respect me. Then forget me."

"Sorry. I'm, just not used this sort of attention." Cupid admitted.

"A good-looking boy like yourself, you've got to be kidding." Gabrielle teased.

"I'm more the, set people up than hook-up kinda guy." Cupid admitted.

"Always the bridesmaid, never the bride." Gabrielle joked.

"You could say that." Cupid realised, laughing nervously.

"So, do you at least find me attractive or am I completely wasting my time with you?" Gabrielle encouraged with a wink.

"How could somebody not fancy you, you're stunning." Cupid confessed.

"There we go. Confidence at last." She said leaning in for a kiss.

Cupid felt the warmth of her lips gently touch down on his before pulling away again. She smiled at him and him at her, then she leaned in for more. She kissed him again and he kissed her back, desperate for a closeness he hadn't felt in such a long time. He felt her tongue breach his lips and he breached hers with his. Then he pulled away suddenly.

"Sorry I can't." Cupid said getting up and leaving the booth.

"What the hell is wrong with you?" Gabrielle asked, chasing after him.

"Sorry, I can taste the blood in your mouth." Cupid admitted.

"What are you on about?" Gabrielle questioned wiping her mouth and looking at her hand to make sure she wasn't bleeding.

"You're a vampire, aren't you?" Cupid questioned.

Gabrielle went quiet. She looked like she had seen a ghost. Cupid went to leave.

"Alright. You're right. I am. But I promise I wasn't going to hurt you. I really am just here to have a good time. How did you know? Are you a hunter?" Gabrielle asked.

"Don't worry, I'm not a hunter. Let's just say I know these things. Look, I'm really sorry about tonight. I didn't mean to offend you. I've got nothing against vamps. I just…"

"…Can't be with one. It's okay. I understand." Gabrielle finished.

"No, that's not it either." Cupid established.

"I didn't ever want to be what I am. But it is who I am now and I can't change that. You have no idea what it's like trying to live your life as something like me."

"Actually I do. I'm an angel." Cupid revealed.

CHAPTER 31

LIFE'S A BEACH

Sandman, the two apprentices and Erika marched out of the temple and over the wooden bridge, constantly glancing over their shoulders as they went. Once they were on the other side of the crossing Sandman stopped.

"Hold hands everyone." Sandman declared putting out his two palms.

Erika and his two apprentices did as they were told and before they knew it, they were in the middle of a desert.

"Where are we?" Erika asked as she took in her new surroundings.

There was thick yellow sand as far as the eye could see in every single direction. There wasn't a single sign of anything else, living or dead.

"Sahara Desert. The golden temple is below us." Sandman answered before floating off in a North-Easterly direction.

"Come on. Keep up." Sandman ordered to the group.

His two apprentices followed him with a brisk walk. Erika ran after them for a hundred metres then gave in, falling to the floor in a heap.

"Just leave me here to die. I deserve it anyway." Erika declared beginning to cry as the day finally started taking its toll on her.

"Nobody deserves to die." Sandman shouted back before floating over to her. "Least of all you."

"I do though. Everything is my fault. It's my fault Santa's dead and it's my fault your two friends are dead and it's my fault the Sins have another gem." Erika huffed.

"Absolute codswallop. The Seven Deadly Sins are the only people to blame for all of this and if we are going to get the gems back, you are going to have to grow up."

Erika did not like his words, but she knew they were true.

"Now hop on." Sandman instructed leaning his back towards her.

"Okay, what's the plan boss?" Erika said, wiping away her tears and climbing onto Sandman's back with a new sense of determination.

"Aldrich, Marilyn. Take Erika's gem and meet me on the Blackpool central pier beach tomorrow at about seven a.m." Sandman ordered.

"Ok. Where are you going?" Aldrich asked as Erika removed the Generosity Gem from her pocket and reluctantly handed it over.

"We are going to find Cupid." Sandman declared before he touched Aldrich and Marilyn on their foreheads making them disappear.

"Hold on." Sandman suggested to Erika before the pair of them disappeared from the desert and found themselves standing in front of the Eiffel Tower.

"Paris!" Erika said excitedly before she noticed they were surrounded by the public, some of whom were already giving the strangely dressed couple some funny looks.

"I think we need some new outfits pronto." Erika suggested as she slid down Sandman's back onto the floor, hoping to

get rid of some of the unwanted
attention they were quickly garnering.

CHAPTER 32

THE CITY OF LOVE

Cupid was stood outside of a posh-looking restaurant looking awkward when a black cab pulled up beside him. Gabrielle got out and paid the driver, before the taxi Parisien pulled away. As she turned around to see Cupid, a huge smirk spread across her face.

"Do you always wear a suit?" Gabrielle joked, looking at his flint coloured three-piece suit.

"Pretty much yeah, why? Do I not suit them?" Cupid asked worryingly.

"Tu es magnifique." Gabrielle said with a grin as she linked his arm and headed toward the restaurant.

"You look beautiful by the way." Cupid said with a smile as they walked through the automatic-doored entranceway.

"Thank you." Gabrielle blushed like a smitten-kitten.

The restaurant itself was a small yet exquisite affair. The brown mahogany walls were lined with numerous paintings housed inside golden frames. Several ice-drop chandeliers hung from the ceiling lighting up the room. A waiter dressed in butler-style attire approached them eagerly.

"Bonjour. Puis-je vous aider?" The waiter asked politely.

"We have a table booked under...?" Gabrielle started.

"...Colin." Cupid put in.

"Ah, the English gentleman. Apologies for my presumptions." The waiter apologised in a French accent. "Please follow me Sir."

The waiter took the pair of them to a table in the corner of the room and pulled out a chair for each of them, placing a folded napkin over their legs.

"Please have a look at the menus. I will return shortly." The waiter gestured before wandering off.

"Colin. Really?" Gabrielle humoured.

"Well I can't use my real name, can I?" Cupid noted.

"Use a pseudonym by all means. But you're not a Colin." Gabrielle said with a giggle.

"Then what am I?" Cupid asked, almost offended.

"You're more of a…" Gabrielle thought for a moment before deciding on "Christian."

"Technically you're right." Cupid laughed. "Fine. In public I'm Christian from now on."

"Can I take your orders Madame, Sir?" The waiter asked, approaching the pair coyishly.

"Chateaubriand Steak with a glass of the house red please."

"How would you like your steak cooked?"

"Rare please."

"Very well. And you Sir?"

"I will get exactly the same, but could I have mine really well done please." Cupid asked politely.

"No problem. Could I get you both anything else?"

"No thanks."

"Very well, enjoy your meal." The waiter finalised before taking the menus from the table and leaving with a bow.

Cupid and Gabrielle had a lovely meal and really enjoyed each other's company. So much so that Cupid didn't want the night to end as they left the restaurant for the cold air outside.

"Would you like to come to my house for a coffee?" Cupid asked hopefully.

"Is that the codeword that boys use now?" Gabrielle said with a grin.

"What do you mean?" Cupid asked with confusion.

"To get a woman back to your flat to try and sleep with her." Gabrielle hinted.

"No, I never. Honestly I wouldn't do that please."

"Cupid I'm kidding. Don't worry, I'd love a coffee." Gabrielle confessed bursting into laughter.

"Oh. Sorry." Cupid blushed.

"Come on. Lead me to your palais." Gabrielle ordered before taking his arm.

CHAPTER 33

TRAINING DAY

Charlie, Samuel, Aoife and the Tooth Fairy had the full woodland to themselves to train in for the day. They split off into pairs with Charlie teaching Sam and Deanne teaching Aoife.

"Right, the training is simple. Try and copy me. Try and keep up with me." Charlie said as he turned into a crow and flew off into the sky.

Samuel closed his eyes and tried to become the hawk again. However, when he opened his eyes, he was looking down at his tattered pair of trainers. He closed his eyes again. This time tighter than before and he concentrated harder than before, but as he re-opened his eyes he was greeted by the same pair of frayed sneakers.

"Come on Sam." Charlie croaked as he circled above the trees of the forest.

"I'm trying." Samuel huffed.

He closed his eyes and began flapping his arms, hoping to emulate the bird he pictured in his mind. He sprung his eyes open, half-expecting to see the same ragged pair of trainers but was surprised to see a set of sharp looking claws.

"Yes." Samuel squawked excitedly, soaring after Charlie who began to zip away from him.

Charlie took a sharp left and flew at full speed. Samuel followed him. Charlie swung a right and soared one hundred feet into the air. Samuel followed with ease. Charlie then dive-bombed past him, picking up speed as he flew toward the surface. Samuel followed, but this time with caution. The floor fast approached the pair as Samuel caught up and got in line with Charlie. They glanced at each other, desperately hoping the other one would pull up first. Twenty feet away and terrified he was going to hit the floor with a thump Sam pulled up. He flapped his wings and watched with worry as Charlie kept going. Fifteen feet, ten feet, five feet. It was then that Charlie leaned back and stretched out one of his wings causing him to spiral into a soft landing on the floor. It was truly majestic sight to watch.

Samuel haphazardly landed next to him and the pair temporarily returned to human form.

"You're not just a kestrel by the way." Charlie informed with amazement.

"What am I?" Samuel asked.

"You're a peregrine falcon. It's only the fastest bird there is." Charlie answered with a grin.

Meanwhile, further inside the forest Aoife and Deanne rolled up their sleeves and removed their wands.

"There's literally millions of different spells available to us. Everything I have taught you up to this point has all been defensive. But where we are going tomorrow you may have to use offensive magick." The Tooth Fairy instructed.

"Like this." Aoife said as she fired a fire bolt out of her wand and scorched a nearby tree.

"Exactly like that. However, I will pretend I just taught you that." The Tooth Fairy informed with a smirk.

"And this." Aoife added as she cast an icicle into the same tree.

"Fine clever clogs. Let's duel and see how much you really know." The Tooth Fairy suggested before she electrocuted Aoife's body causing her to fall into a small puddle with a plop.

"I will get you back for that Deanne." Aoife said flying after her.

The pair zapped all sorts of weird and wonderful spells at each other. Most of them missing their target and hitting nearby trees and bushes. At one point the pair of them had to work together to put out a fire as one of Aoife's spells hit a gathering of leaves causing them to burst into flames.

"You're pretty good. Not much to teach you after all." The Tooth Fairy admitted as she caught her breath.

"Thanks. I picked up a little bit here and there."

"There are two more spells that might come in handy though. But you have to promise you won't teach either of them to any of the other fairies.

"Right."

"I mean it Aoife. Promise me." The Tooth Fairy reiterated.

"Okay. I promise. Just teach me the spell."

The Tooth Fairy whispered into Aoife's ear as if she was scared of the very trees hearing her words.

"Right. And what does that do?" Aoife asked with intrigue.

"This." The Tooth Fairy announced before she pointed the wand toward her own body and cast the spell.

Suddenly she began to grow exponentially, higher and higher until she was the height of a full-sized human being. Aoife couldn't believe her eyes. She flew around her frantically taking-in the full height of her six-foot tall friend with amazement.

"That's amazing Deanne." Aoife adored.

As the rustling of leaves approached them both, Deanne turned the wand on herself and cast another spell causing her to quickly shrink back down to her normal fairy-sized self.

"I think we are done for the day. How about you's?" Charlie asked the pair as he found them.

"Yeah us too." Deanne said with a sly wink to Aoife.

CHAPTER 34

CHRISTMAS CRACKERS

Jasper, Anya, Ollie, Mollie and Zwarte ate in complete silence as they worked their way through a mountain of cauliflowers, sprouts and potatoes. Anya watched to make sure everyone had stopped eating before she got up and cleared the table. When she returned she looked positively determined.

"Right, are we going to mope about all day or are we gonna do something about the Seven Deadly Sins and Jack Frost?" Anya snapped in a Russian accent.

"I agree. We should go get our gems back so our families haven't died for noffing." Mollie squeaked.

"And I think I know where they are." Jasper put in.

"Where?" Ollie drummed.

"Ianua Temple." Jasper answered sharply as if the words themselves hurt his lips as they left his mouth.

"Impossible. Jack O'Lantern died destroying the temple with Belphegor inside." Zwarte corrected.

"I thought that too, but then I remembered the door."

"What door?" Mollie questioned.

"The seven gems, the ones that we were all supposed to protect. They open a door inside Ianua Temple. Without the door they are useless. And there's no other way passed the door because it's...

"...Indestructible. Belphegor must have got near the door and survived." Zwarte realised.

"What's inside the door?" Anya asked.

"A treasure chest." Jasper answered.

"And inside the treasure chest?" Anya pressed.

"The Hell Sphere." Jasper confirmed.

"What the Hell is that?" Ollie asked.

"It's basically a sphere that would allow the Devil to march his entire army to Earth." Zwarte put in.

"The devil's actually real?" Mollie asked with surprise.

"Yes. So, we have to try and stop them, whatever the cost." Jasper warned.

"Fine, we all go together." Anya simplified.

"We can't. Some of us will have to stay and look after the animals. We might have to evacuate them all over again if the Sins come here." Jasper informed.

"Crackers." Ollie announced loudly.

"What?" Anya questioned.

"We pull crackers for it. The winners go to Ianua temple. The losers stay behind for the animals." Ollie suggested waving one of the crackers about.

"I think me, my Dad and Zwarte should go. The rest of you should stay behind. It's dangerous." Anya suggested.

"No. He is right. It is the only fair way of doing it." Jasper concluded. "Whoever gets the party hat in their cracker piece, gets to go."

"You're not missing us out." Mollie argued.

"Fine. Is everyone in agreement?" Zwarte asked gathering several crackers together on the table.

The sound of someone coughing from behind him almost made Zwarte jump out of his skin. As he turned around there were two small elves standing to attention.

"Hi. We heard you speaking and we would like to help you on your mission." The elf requested.

"I don't think that's a good idea I'm afraid. It's really dangerous where we are going." Zwarte dismissed.

"But if they win and get the Hell Sphere it will be dangerous for all elves everywhere. Please let us help." The elf reiterated.

"They have a point. Give them a cracker." Jasper instructed.

Zwarte reluctantly handed a silver cracker over. The two elves shared it before yanking at the same time causing the cracker to snap with a bang. They both looked inside their own halves before one of them pulled out an orange party hat revealing himself to be the victor.

"Okay Zwarte and Anya. You're next." Jasper suggested handing them a golden cracker.

"Ready?" Anya asked before yanking at the cracker with determination. She was disappointed as Zwarte revealed a red party hat inside his half of the cracker.

"Ollie and Mollie." Jasper said handing over a red cracker.

The two giant bunnies pulled at the same time causing the Christmas cracker to snap with a bang. They both searched their cracker halves together. Mollie pulled out a green party hat to reveal she was going.

"That's it then. It is decided. We leave tomorrow." Jasper informed.

"You haven't pulled a cracker yet. I should pull with you." Anya suggested trying to thrust a cracker into her Dad's hand.

"I'm the only one here that knows where Ianua temple is, so I go by default." Jasper decided before walking from the room.

CHAPTER 35

CUPID'S HOME

"You ready for the tour?" Cupid asked as he unlocked his front door and let Gabrielle inside.

"Yeah." Gabrielle said excitedly, walking into his sitting room.

The room was quite ordinary looking. A little on the minimalist side for her liking, but nice and tidy. Gabrielle had an inkling the entire inside of the house was going to be painted bright pink. She was really glad it wasn't.

"Can I ask you a question?" Cupid asked.

"Yeah sure." Gabrielle replied with a nervous smile.

"Cos you're a vampire, do I have to invite you in every time you come here, or will just the once do?"

Gabrielle burst into laughter.

"That's not actually a real thing with us. I could sneak into your house and bite you anytime I want. Invited or not." Gabrielle teased with a wink.

"Okay just checking." Cupid smiled.

"Come on then. Give me this tour you promised." Gabrielle pressed.

"So, this is the sitting room slash kitchen obviously..." Cupid started before walking to a corridor with three doors.

"...This is the bathroom." Cupid said, opening one of the doors to reveal a small white room that was equipped with a bath, shower, sink and toilet.

Gabrielle popped her head inside to have a quick look. When she was done Cupid closed the door behind her.

"...This is the closet." Cupid said revealing a small box room with multiple cleaning devices inside. At the bottom of the room there was a small black box. Gabrielle went in for a closer look.

"What's in the box?" Gabrielle asked with intrigue.

"Long story." Cupid said, shutting the door promptly.

"Well I wanna know now!"

"Sorry I'd rather not talk about it if that's okay?" Cupid petitioned.

"Okay fair enough." Gabrielle said, walking for the final door.

"And this is the bedroom." Cupid announced revealing a small room containing a bed, a wardrobe and a couple of bedside cabinets.

The plain bedroom with its tidy complexion and made-bed gave the impression that Cupid's house was more like a show-home than somewhere that was actually lived in.

"So, this is where the magick happens?" Gabrielle asked, sitting on the edge of the bed and testing the springs.

"I do magick in every room, not just this one." Cupid corrected.

"I was joking. It's a saying." Gabrielle informed with a smile.

"I know. I was kidding also." Cupid chuckled.

"Come here you." Gabrielle directed, tapping the bed next to her.

Cupid went and sat beside her on the edge of the bed. He had no idea what to do or say.

"I erm..." Cupid started.

"Shhh." Gabrielle ordered, leaning in for a kiss.

Cupid closed his eyes and kissed her back. What started as a soft loving kiss quickly escalated to something fast and passionate. They stood up together, never parting their lips, their hands all over each other's bodies. As Gabrielle began to remove Cupid's blazer there was a pounding knock at the door.

Gabrielle pulled away annoyed.

"Just ignore it." Cupid suggested throwing his blazer across the room and pulling her back in.

Gabrielle pressed herself against him. Unbuttoning his shirt as they passionately kissed. The knock at the boor became overwhelmingly loud and more frantic. As if somebody was in desperate need of help.

"Be right back." Cupid said marching from the room and toward the front door.

Just as he was about to answer it, the door was kicked through, falling onto the floor with a dull thud.

"Hello Cupid." Pride declared walking into the room with his brothers and sisters in tow, Jack Frost entering in last place like an unwanted servant.

CHAPTER 36

RUPERT CLAUS

Nova Claus walked carefully through a darkened cavern with her wand at the ready. She swung it side to side as if something was about to jump out from the darkness either side of her. As she turned full circle, she stood on something that clicked underneath her foot. She swallowed her panic and looked down to see what it was. A grey sigil was glowing on the floor below her. Before Nova had a chance to react her feet suddenly turned to stone before the spell worked its way right up her body freezing her like concrete to the floor.

It was at least an hour she stood there waiting for something to happen before she eventually heard a whistling noise approaching her. The familiar Christmas tune was music to her ears.

"MMMM!" Was all her muffled cries could muster.

"Hello?" A voice called out into the darkness.

"MMMMMM!" Nova cried louder as a shadowy figure entered the room.

It was a man with a long brown beard wearing a long brown duffel coat. He looked at her statued form with intrigue before he removed a small yellow tape and began checking out her measurements.

"Mmmmmm. Mm'm. Mm." Nova tried.

"Argh. I see." The man declared before removing his wand and zapping Nova's body.

She was relieved as the stone surrounding her entire frame began to disappear, allowing her to move again.

"Thank you. I thought I was gonna be stuck there forever."

"What are you doing here Nova?" The bearded-man asked before walking off.

"I've got something I need to tell you." Nova said, hanging her head as she remembered. She followed him as she thought about how she was going to break the news.

"Fine. You've got the time it takes me to drink a brew and then I want you gone." The man declared as he opened a circular doorway for her.

Nova walked inside to a warmth she hadn't felt in a while. The big circular room was a mix of different rooms. There was a bed in one far corner, a toilet and sink in the opposite corner. A mini fridge and table to the near left of her and a small portable television to her right. In the centre of the room there was a big coal fire heating everything up.

The man bent over and picked up a small metal shovel from the hearth and collected several pieces of coal from a mound not far from the fire. He threw it on the fire and stoked it with the shovel before shunting the metal fireguard back in its place with his left boot. He then removed his gloves and boiled the kettle. When it whistled its completion, he made himself a mug of tea and made Nova a malted milk.

"Why did you leave the North Pole Uncle Rupert?" Nova asked before sipping her drink.

"Me and your Dad had a bit of an argument and I thought it was best that I left."

"What over?" Nova asked.

"You best ask him love." Rupert dismissed.

"But I want you to tell me." Nova insisted.

"I don't think that's a good idea. I don't wanna bring up the past."

"Please. I need to know." Nova spurred.

Rupert fell silent as if he was scared of what he was going to say. He got up, removed his coat and hung it up before sitting back down.

"Your Dad and I have different views of the world and the people in it."

Rupert started before taking a deep breath.

"We all know that." Nova admitted.

"Well, when your Mum died of cancer, I felt like he should be there for you. Me, Jasper and Anya said we would take on all the Christmas duties so he could concentrate on you."

"But he wouldn't take a back seat." Nova realised.

"No. If anything he took on more than usual, and then he sent away Zwarte cos he was worried about him offending people. And that's when I confronted him again."

"And what happened?" Nova pushed.

"I complained that he cares more about the stupid human children than he does about his own daughter. And then I punched him." Rupert admitted, his cheeks glowing red with embracement.

"You actually punched him?" Nova asked with a shocked giggle.

"Yeah. I apologised immediately and goaded him to hit me back. But he wouldn't." Rupert confessed.

"What did he do?"

"He said 'I think it's best you leave Rupert'." Rupert said in a mocking voice which caused the pair of them to giggle into silence.

"What did you really come here for?" Rupert eventually asked.

"There is something bad I've come to tell you." Nova started.

CHAPTER 37

THE LOVE GEM

Cupid looked through the unwanted guests with a mystified annoyance. Jack Frost was the only face he recognised so he ignored the rest of them and addressed him personally.

"Jack. Who are your friends and what are you all doing here? Now isn't a good time." Cupid implored.

"Give us the Love Gem and we will leave immediately." Greed suggested.

"Don't be silly. Jack knows I can't just give you it. Now, can you all please leave before I have to remove you." Cupid threatened.

"Cupid please just give us the gem. We don't want to hurt you." Jack pleaded.

"You don't stand a chance against us, not when you're all alone." Envy teased.

"But he's not alone." A woman's voice corrected as she walked into the room.

A smile spread across Cupid's face as Gabby arrived and wrapped her arms around him.

"Fatty. Come here." Jack suggested to Sloth who quickly approached him.

"We will keep him busy. You and Sophie look for the gem." Jack suggested before walking up to Cupid. "I'm sorry about this." Jack Frost suggested before he held out the palm of his hands and began to freeze a wall of solid ice locking Cupid and Gabrielle inside.

Cupid shrugged his shoulders, pulled a bow out of thin air and fired an arrow into the ice causing the full wall to shatter and fall to the floor. Jack looked shocked.

"Sisters, get the girl. We will handle Cupid." Pride suggested before removing his retractable sword from its sheath and charging at Cupid.

Cupid deflected all of Pride's strikes with the limbs of his bow while Envy, Lust and Gluttony made their way around the sparing pair to get to Gabrielle. Gluttony was first to get there and grabbed Gabrielle's arm with a grin. The grin disappeared as Gabrielle broke free and then threw her large frame out of the window with ease. Lust and Envy looked at each other with surprised confusion.

"You aren't human." Envy seethed.

"Neither are you." Gabrielle winked before swinging a punch toward her.

Cupid took a strike from behind that knocked him to the floor. While he was down Wrath kicked him in the face bursting his nose and busting his lip at the same time.

"Mind if I join in?" A man in a pair of blue jeans and yellow t-shirt asked from the doorway.

The remaining Sins glanced around nervously. But only Jack and Cupid recognised the man immediately.

"Sandman." Cupid confirmed with a relieved smile.

"Come on Wrath." Pride called out walking toward the Sandman with an excited bounce.

Sandman dodged Pride's sword and Wrath's baseball bat with ease, ending up in the middle of the room. He kicked Jack onto the sofa and pulled Cupid back to his feet before he grabbed a nearby curtain and wrapped Wrath's head inside slamming him blindly to the floor. He was about to stamp on his head when a voice stopped his foot in mid-air.

"I wouldn't if I were you." Envy shouted into the room.

As everyone turned around, they noticed a worn-out looking Envy with a knife to Gabrielle's neck.

"If anyone moves, she's dead." Envy threatened.

"No please." Cupid pleaded dropping his bow to the floor.

"The gem for the girl. Simples." Envy proposed.

"Don't do it Cupid." Sandman suggested.

Cupid took no notice of Sandman and pulled the Love Gem out of thin air, it sparkled as he handed it over to Pride. Sandman looked disappointed but didn't protest anymore. Sloth, Sophie Stork and Jack Frost all left Cupid's home quickly. The others deliberately bumped into Sandman as they left with an arrogant pride, except Envy who stood with her knife still pressed to Gabrielle's neck.

"Please let her go." Cupid begged desperately.

"Very well." Envy said with a smile before slicing the blade along the width of Gabrielle's neck tearing it open.

"Nooooo." Cupid cried running over to her as the blood began gushing from the open wound in her neck.

Sandman was in shock and did nothing as Envy ran past him cackling an unwarranted laughter.

CHAPTER 38

SETTING THE TRAP

The Seven Deadly Sins returned to Ianua temple looking positively accomplished. Wrath and Gluttony less so with their superficial injuries.

"Did you get the gem?" Belphegor asked excitedly.

"Yes. Here." Pride said throwing it over to him.

Belphegor grabbed it and approached the door with exhilaration. He hastily fumbled the gem inside a slot. As it glowed its acceptance he stood back and looked on the door with a new sense of veneration.

"One more to go. Time to lay the trap." Belphegor demanded with a twinkle in his eye.

"Come here you." Pride said, grabbing Sophie Stork by the arm causing her to scream.

"Get off her. She is mine." Sloth stipulated, pushing Pride away.

"Let go of her fatty." Jack Frost demanded, squaring up to Sloth.

Sloth reluctantly let go of her, but bent down and whispered into her ear.

"Don't worry. I won't let any of them hurt you."

"Ooooo. You've changed your tune Jack. I like it." Belphegor put in with a round of applause. "As a favour to you, I'm going to release the last of your sisters."

"Don't do it. He will betray us the second she is free." Lust advised.

"He wouldn't dare. Besides, we need someone to pass the message on." Belphegor informed.

"Sitri!" Belphegor shouted into the room.

"Yes sir." Sitri said rushing into the room with a ridiculous sense of obedience.

"Release Jack's sister and demand her to tell the other Festives that we will trade the kid for the last gem at the North York Moors." Belphegor instructed.

"Very well, Sir." Sitri said, rushing from the room.

*****

Jasmine Stump was a twiglet of a girl. She had long knobbly knees, and long knobbly elbows and her fingers looked like misshapen breadsticks. She wore barely any clothes around her albino skin and was probably only kept warm by the mane of ginger hair that hung the length of her body. Her most distinguishing feature was the pair of small bare twigs that grew from her head like antlers.

She was sat blowing the orange leaves that had gathered in her personal prison, when there was a bang against the cell door.

"Stand in the corner Autumn." A voice demanded before unlocking the door.

"Hand out." Sitri demanded as he entered her cell with two fellow daemons.

Jasmine had found out the hard way that it was easier to obey the rules than to break them so she did as she was told. She felt the corners of a scrunched-up piece of paper placed onto her palm before she felt a strike to the face. She stood up in anger ready to fight back when she realised the prison walls were gone, replaced by a familiar Scottish setting.

*****

When Sitri returned to the temple, he found himself in front of fifteen faces he didn't recognise.

"Who are all of these daemons, Sir?" Sitri asked.

"The reinforcements I sent for. Take ten of them to the moors with you. Leave five with me to help protect the temple in

case they try anything." Belphegor
ordered.

CHAPTER 39

MISTLETOE AND WINE

Jasper began looking through his supplies box for anything that could be used as a weapon.

"Aha." He said as he pulled out what looked like a century old bottle of wine. He ran over to the small elf and handed it over.

"Drink this. It will make you invisible."

The elf took a large swig of the wine, before the bottle seemingly floated back into Jasper's hand.

"Did it work?" A voice asked from somewhere in the room.

"It appears so." Jasper said with a grin.

"When we get there, you should be able to slip through the battle unnoticed and grab the gems. It's my guess they will be attached to a door somewhere within the temple."

"Consider it done." A voice declared from right next to him making Jasper jump in his boots.

Jasper rushed back to the chest to rifle through some more of its contents. Eventually he found a piece of Mistletoe and grabbed it happily.

"Mollie. Take this." Jasper said, pushing it into her paws.

"I'm supposed to fight the Seven Deadly Sins with a crappy old piece of Mistletoe. Thanks a bunch." Mollie joked.

"This isn't Mistletoe. It's anti-mistletoe." Jasper announced excitedly.

"What the hell is anti-mistletoe?" Ollie squalled with laughter.

"Kicking someone under anti-mistletoe makes them uncontrollably angry." Anya answered.

"Why do I want to make them angrier?" Mollie asked with worry.

"Cos if you kick a few of them, they will end up fighting each other in order to get to you." Jasper informed, laughing at the thought.

"Is everyone ready?" Jasper asked picking up his wand and two Rubik's cubes.

"Mollie..." Ollie said, hopping over to his sister. "...Please be careful."

The two human-sized rabbits squeezed each other in a furry hug.

"I will." Mollie said, kissing him on the cheek.

Jasper walked outside into the forest and threw a solved Rubik's cube onto the cold snow. It un-winded itself into a portal that Zwarte, Jasper, Anya, Mollie and the invisible elf walked through. On the other side they found themselves in a different forest entirely.

"Remember. Anyone who comes through that isn't us throw the bauble into the air and run back through the portal. Once the bauble smashes…" Jasper started.

"…It'll close both portals, I know." Anya finished.

"Any problems just evacuate everybody and we will find you all later."

Jasper instructed before hugging his daughter.

"Don't worry about me, I'll be fine. Now go get them gems back." Anya ordered before breaking free and punching her Dad in the shoulder.

"Room for two more?" A voice asked from deeper in the forest causing everyone to turn on edge.

They watched with panic as two figures entered their field of vision. A woman in red and a man in a long brown coat.

"So, that's where you went." Zwarte said with a smile as he realised who it was.

"Rupert. It's so good to see you. I, erm, have something to tell you." Jasper started.

"Don't worry. Nova has filled me in on everything and I'm here to help." Rupert updated.

"You'll help us get the gems back?" Jasper asked with surprise.

"No. You guys can concentrate on the gems you lost. I'm only here for one thing."

"What's that?" Mollie asked.

"Revenge." Rupert declared through gritted teeth.

"Fair enough. Is everybody ready?" Jasper asked.

Murmurs of agreement told Jasper it was time. He solved the Rubik's cube and threw it onto the leaf-scattered earth. It opened itself into a portal and the group could see inside the Ianua temple. The group weren't all mentally prepared and ready for what they were walking into, but they no longer had a choice.

CHAPTER 40

ATTACK ON IANUA TEMPLE

Charlie and Sam had the most unusual of breakfasts. It was essentially mushrooms on toast. But the bread tasted sweet and the mushrooms tasted bitter. None the less, they were hungry and the food filled them sufficiently. Aoife and Deanne cleared their plates before they all made their way outside.

"You sure you are both ready for this?" Deanne asked.

"Yes." Charlie and Sam said together.

"And you Aoife? It's not too late to change your mind." The Tooth Fairy advised.

"We have to do this. Together." Aoife announced.

"Very well. Everyone hold hands." The Tooth Fairy ordered stretching out her tiny fingers.

The group all held hands forming a perfect circle. As Deanne sneezed the four of them disappeared and found themselves inside the walls of the Ianua Temple. The five daemons that were sitting around looking bored inside didn't even notice their arrival.

"Aoife. Sam. That's the door. Go." The Tooth Fairy pointed out before she removed her wand and cast a spell into the centre of the room. Out of thin air a giant wasp's nest appeared and fell to the floor with a crash.

"They're here." Belphegor announced to the room with an excited smile.

The daemons turned their attention to the new arrivals and charged towards the group with a bloodthirsty desire to prove themselves. Fortunately, the group of pissed off wasps had other plans and began to fill the room with a buzzing sense of revenge.

Samuel sprouted his pinions and took off around the outside of the room. Heading toward the door that the Tooth Fairy had pointed out. Aoife flapped her tiny wings and went the opposite way around the temple.

"Hop on." Charlie instructed as he shrunk down into a crow.

Deanne jumped on his back and began firing spells at the daemons as Charlie circled the room.

With their visibility distracted by the swarm of indignant wasps the daemons were pretty much useless. Belphegor put out his hands either side of his body and clapped a thunderous blow which sent everything in the air against the nearest wall. The wasps, the Storks and the fairies all smashed against stone with a thud.

Samuel jumped back onto his claws and quickly darted for the door. But as he neared it, he was grabbed by something that felt like a whip. He struggled free before he was struck by something, hitting the nearest wall with a bigger thud than before. It winded him more than he could contemplate and it forced him back into his human form.

Aoife got up and flew for the door, dodging every daemon that lunged for her with relative ease. She arrived safely and yanked at one of the six glistening gems. Before she managed to prize it free a long tail wrapped itself around her like a snake and began to crush her tiny frame.

"Argh." She screamed in agony as Charlie flew toward her to try and break her free. One of the daemons managed to land a blow to the side of his head before he got there causing him to hit the floor with a crash.

The Tooth Fairy jumped up and cast a spell straight at Belphegor causing him to drop Aoife in order to dodge it.

"Are you okay?" Deanne asked as she scooped the fairy up from the floor and flew to the edge of the room.

"Yeah. But I don't think we can win." Aoife suggested with disappointment.

CHAPTER 41

THIRST FOR BLOOD.

Cupid tried to stem the bleeding on Gabrielle's neck as best as he could while Sandman just stood there in shock. As her brown skin began to flush lighter in colour Cupid knew he had no other choice.

"Gabby. You have to bite me and drink my blood." Cupid suggested.

"I can't." Gabby protested, choking and coughing on the blood that was accumulating in her throat.

"If you die, I will kill myself. You have to do it." Cupid ordered, freeing up the area around his neck before pulling her head in.

Gabby didn't want to feed on him. She knew it would change things between them and she loved what they had. But she also knew the only alternative was death. She opened her mouth, revealing a sharp-looking set of fangs and bit into Cupid's delicious-looking neck.

She sucked with all the strength she had left, swallowing his red ichor each time her mouth filled up. Her throat warmed as she drank and drank and drank. After a few long minutes, Sandman began to worry about the amount she had already taken and approached the pair with caution.

"I think that is enough." Sandman recommended.

"No…" Cupid protested, putting his hand in the way of Sandman. "…Let her take what she needs."

Gabby was clearly gaining in strength as her body rose from its limp lying state to a more dominant kneeling stance over Cupid's body. It was Cupid who was now looking worse for wear. His already pale skin was beginning to look cold and clammy.

"Please, stop." Sandman implored.

Gabby ignored his request and continued drinking.

"Stop. Now." Sandman ordered placing his hand on her shoulder.

Gabby jumped up and threw him across the length of the room, before sinking her teeth back into Cupid's bloody neck.

"I'm glad you're okay." Cupid whispered with a smile as he noticed her neck had completely recovered.

As Sandman sprung back to his feet and marched across the room, he was pleased to see Gabby had reluctantly pulled herself away from Cupid. It looked like her body wanted to continue drinking but her brain was the one resisting. She screamed at the top of her lungs before retreating from the room.

"Are you okay?" Sandman asked holding Cupid's hand.

"I will be now." Cupid smiled before passing out.

It was two hours later when Cupid finally woke back up. He wasn't sure if his eyes were deceiving him, but he was sure that Sandman was standing talking to a really small woman.

"Hello." Cupid said, alerting the pair to his conscious presence.

"Welcome back." Sandman said, rushing over.

"How is Gabby?" Cupid asked as his memory began returning to him.

"Alive. She had to stop herself from draining you completely and then she ran off screaming." Sandman answered honestly.

"Good. Do you think you could help me get my gem back now please?" Cupid asked.

"About that. We have some catching up to do first." Sandman declared before helping Cupid to his feet.

CHAPTER 42

FESTIVES VS DAEMONS

Belphegor grabbed the Tooth Fairy and bowled her at the nearest wall like a cricket ball before volleying Charlie away like a football. Aoife charged at him angrily, but she was rapidly back-handed away. Samuel tried to scratch Belphegor's eyes with his talons but he was grabbed by the beast's whippet tail and threw against the ground.

"Hey scar face. Pick on someone your own size." Jasper Claus suggested before throwing a spherule of tinsel at Belphegor, which wrapped itself around his feet causing Belphegor to hit the floor with a nasty crash.

Four of the five daemons in the room approached the new arrivals, while one attempted to keep Samuel and Aoife away from the door. They could both get past the female daemon with ease, but they both struggled to wriggle free any of the gems from the door, before they were swatted away.

As the group of daemons neared them, Rupert pulled out a small handgun and shot one of the daemons square in the head killing it instantly. Before he had a chance to fire another round a daemon appeared behind him and clonked him over the head with a piece of rock causing Rupert to keel over and drop the gun.

Mollie turned around and drop-kicked the daemon across the length of the room before she was grabbed by a different one and pulled away by her neck.

"Help get the gems." Jasper instructed to the invisible elf pointing to the door, before helping his brother up from the floor.

"Me and Zwarte will deal with the daemons. You keep Belphegor busy." Nova suggested as she pulled out her wand and slammed one of the daemons against the ceiling and another one against a wall. As Rupert and Jasper approached Belphegor, one of the daemons grabbed Zwarte and disappeared out of the room. As he managed to break free, he found himself falling from the clouds, one-hundred-feet above the temple and descending rapidly.

Meanwhile, Mollie was getting choked to death in the corner of the room by one of the daemons.

"How do you like it?" A fully-grown Charlie asked grabbing the daemon in an arm lock and strangling it. The daemon spun lose and slapped Charlie to the floor. He was about to kick him in the face when the daemon suddenly flew across the room.

"We are even." Mollie said with a giggle, before offering Charlie a furry paw to help him back to his feet.

They were both forced to quickly shrink into their smaller forms as a huge column flew through the air toward them. It smashed into a thousand pieces and shook the entire temple around them. The haphazard scaffolding was now the only thing keeping the temple intact.

Belphegor deflected or dodged all of Jasper's spells as he approached the man, wrapping his long tail around Jasper's body and throwing him across the length of the room. Nova (who was busy wrestling with one of the daemons) noticed her Uncle flying through the air and just managed to wedge herself between Jasper and the wall before he hit it.

"Dodge this." Rupert said confidently as he began firing a series of different coloured and sized snakes out the end of his wand. Belphegor managed to throw away or kill the majority of them. However, a Black Mamba and a brown Philippine Cobra both managed to inject some venom into the daemon, slowing down his speedy onslaught.

Sensing her opportunity Mollie removed her anti-mistletoe and began landing blows left, right and centre. She even landed one on the mighty Belphegor himself, who furiously ran after her like a train roaring into a station. Nova, Deanne and Jasper tried their best to keep

Belphegor and the daemons off her back as she retreated through the room.

Meanwhile, the female daemon was so busy swatting at Aoife and Samuel that she hadn't even noticed that an invisible elf had managed to grab a chair and was gleefully pulling a third gem out of its slot in the door. However, one of the other daemons had noticed the idle chair standing against the door, with a gem mysteriously floating above it.

The daemon skipped to the door with urgency, frantically looking around for the culprit. It didn't take him long to locate the invisible elf who was merrily singing to himself on the chair. The daemon picked up his invisible body and snapped it with a sharp crunch. The Life Gem, Dream Gem and the Laughter Gem all fell to the floor with a ping.

CHAPTER 43

FAMILIAR FACES

In the corner of the temple, Sam swooped over and grabbed the Life Gem with his beak while Aoife zoomed across and grabbed the Dream Gem with her tiny hands. The daemon that snapped the elf in two grabbed the remaining Laughter Gem and stuck it back inside the door. It glowed red as it confirmed its place.

In the centre of the room Belphegor was chasing Mollie around attempting to catch her with a clap, like a human might catch a fly. As more daemons began to appear out of nowhere, Jasper, Nova, Rupert, Deanne and Charlie struggled to keep them at bay. They were fighting a losing battle.

Meanwhile, Zwarte Piet was five seconds away from death. He had dropped his wand inside the temple and he was about to hit the cold hard temple roof with a crunch. He closed his eyes, expecting death to imminently follow.

"Hold on." A familiar voice yelled, grabbing his hand and stopping his fall.

As Zwarte was carefully put down on the temple roof he looked up to see who had saved his life. He was pleasantly surprised to see the familiar faces of Sandman and Cupid.

"About time you two showed up. Everybody else is already here." Zwarte said with a smile.

"Better late than never." Sandman said with a wink, grabbing them both and pulling them through the solid concrete roof of the temple, as if it wasn't there.

Charlie was suddenly grabbed mid-flight and pinned down by his wings. As he squawked for help, one of the daemons pulled out a knife and was about to cut him in two when an arrow went straight through the daemon's head and into a nearby wall. As the other daemon spun around to see who had killed his friend, he too was felled by an arrow. The daemon fell to the floor in a heap, revealing Cupid as Charlie's saviour.

As Jasper was dis-wanded and held in place by two daemons, he could do nothing as a third daemon began smacking him in the face. Each vicious strike was like being hit with a brick. After several painful blows he hoped the next one would put him out of his misery. But it didn't arrive. He strained a look through his puffed-out eyeballs and managed to make out Zwarte Piet and Nova coming to his aid.

Mollie shrunk down in size to run in-between a daemon's legs before growing again to hop over another. But she wasn't quick enough and Belphegor finally managed to grab her. He began squeezing her fluffy soft frame with a grin as she felt her wee arms crunching under his brute strength. She grunted in agony. The pain stopped as quickly as it had started and she felt herself hit the floor with a thump as Belphegor let go of her. Mollie looked over with admiration as she saw a scrawny man with flimsy-looking features pulling Belphegor across the room by his tail.

"Who is that?" Mollie asked.

"Mr Sandman." Deanne confirmed, helping Mollie back to her paws.

"Isn't he just beautiful?" Mollie said dreamily.

"I'm more of a Jack Frost fan myself." Deanne blushed.

"Don't move, either of you." Pride ordered as he rested his sword on Mollie's shoulder.

"Drop the wand slut!" Envy said with a giggle as she grabbed Deanne and put a knife to her neck.

The Tooth Fairy did as she was told and looked to Jack for help as Charlie and Zwarte were also grabbed and pulled to one side.

"It's over. Drop your weapons everybody!" Greed shouted into the temple.

The chaos of the ongoing battle ceased immediately as everyone looked to one another for direction. Everybody stood still and paid attention, but nobody dropped their weapons.

"If you want your friends to live, you will all do as you're told." Greed suggested.

"If you want your boss to live, you will do as you are told." Sandman countered, his arm wrapped tightly around Belphegor's neck.

"Sophie." Samuel realised, shifting from his bird form back into a human.

"Sammy?" Sophie asked with surprise. Rubbing her eyes to make sure she had just seen a bird turn into her brother.

"Don't worry. Everything is gonna be alright." Sam promised.

"Shut up you." Greed suggested

CHAPTER 44

STALEMATE

The Seven Deadly Sins glanced around the room nervously. While they were busy capturing Deanne, Mollie, Zwarte and Charlie. The Festives had captured some of the daemons including Sitri and Belphegor.

"Ah. It seems we have a stalemate then." Greed said with a grin.

"Tell them to give up my friends." Sandman ordered, tightening his grip around Belphegor's neck.

"Noooo." Belphegor groaned painfully.

It was then that Jack Frost spotted Rupert's handgun lying idle on the floor.

He picked it up by the barrel and inspected it curiously.

"What should we do?" Lust asked Greed for direction.

"Here take this. If that child moves without my permission. Shoot her." Jack proposed as he handed the gun over to Pride. It was cold to the touch, like it had been kept in a fridge.

"What are you doing Jack?" Greed seethed through gritted teeth.

"I have a plan. Trust me." Jack declared, budging him out of the way.

"You fuck this up, you're dead." Greed promised.

"Daemons, Festives!!!" Jack shouted into the room to get its full attention. "You both have reasons for hating me. And rightly so. But I am going to make a deal today that everyone will be happy with."

Jack grabbed Deanne and Mollie and led them away from their captives to the other end of the room. Pride and Envy watched with intrigue.

"Sandman, release Belphegor. Rupert, release Sitri." Jack suggested.

"I do not trust you." Sandman publicised, his grip resolute.

"Then people will die unnecessarily." Jack Frost reasoned.

"Like Stork you mean." Charlie shouted.

"And my Uncle." Mollie seethed.

"And my Dad." Nova spat angrily.

"I am sorry about all that business. I truly am. But if you don't make this trade now, more will die." Jack proposed. "Please Sandman. Release Belphegor."

"Trust me." He thought, hoping Sandman was reading his mind.

Sandman looked frustrated but released his grip. Belphegor and Sitri scuttled away gratefully.

"That was a fair trade. Now, give us the three remaining gems and I will give you the three remaining prisoners." Jack proposed as he eyed Zwarte, Charlie and Sophie.

Samuel didn't think twice before handing over the Life Gem to Jack. Lust was then forced to release Charlie.

Aoife reluctantly flew over to Jack and handed over the Dream Gem and in turn Wrath grudgingly released Zwarte Piet.

"The Generosity Gem please Jasper." Jack Frost urged.

"I haven't got it Jack. I swear." Jasper pleaded as Sloth tightened his grip around Sophie Stork.

"The gem for the girl Jasper." Jack proposed.

"I promise you, I don't know where it is." Jasper implored.

"Fine, Rupert?" Jack redirected.

"No idea sorry." Rupert admitted.

"Well one of you must know where the bleeding thing is." Jack shouted in frustration.

The room fell quiet.

"Fine, kill Sophie Stork." Jack suggested.

Pride aimed the gun at Sophie Stork who instantly burst into tears, fearing for her life.

"WAIT!" Sandman announced, before Pride could pull the trigger. "I have it. Give me a minute."

Sandman disappeared into thin air.

"What should we do?" Mollie asked feeling redundant on the other side of the room.

"Nothing yet." Deanne advised.

It took Sandman more than the minute he had promised to return in, but when he did return, he had the Generosity Gem in his hand. He reluctantly handed it over to Jack.

"The girl." Sandman demanded, putting out his hand.

"She stays where she is 'til we have tested the gems. I'm sure you understand." Jack announced as he handed the missing gems to Belphegor.

"Well done Jack." Belphegor congratulated with a twinkle in his eye.

CHAPTER 45

END GAME

Belphegor gleefully placed the gems into the door which shone a glowing red before squeaking open to reveal a small treasure chest. He picked up the crimson trunk and disappeared out of the room along with all of the other daemons, leaving the Festives and the Seven Deadly Sins alone.

"Well done Jack. You just ended the world." Sandman declared in anger.

"No, I haven't. Don't be so temperamental." Jack Frost said with an accomplished smile. "Now come here Fatty."

Sloth grabbed hold of Sophie Stork's hand and walked toward Jack Frost with worry.

"Do you remember what I told you before Sloth?" Jack said with a tear in his eye.

"Yeah." Sloth said with a blank expression on his face.

"We discussed a plan, SLOTH!!!" Jack reiterated, hoping he would remember their pact.

"Yeah but. Oh..." Sloth started, before he realised that Jack had called him by his real name. Sloth picked up Sophie Stork and made a run for the Festives at the other end of the room. Lust tried to run after them both but Jack Frost tripped her using the long icicle he had forged into his right hand. Pride aimed his gun at the little girls bobbing head and pulled the trigger. Nothing happened. The guns internal mechanism was frozen solid.

"You bastard." Pride said dropping the gun to the floor. He pulled out his sword and swung it at Jack's head but he disappeared into thin air before he had a chance to land the blow.

Greed and Wrath were next to disappear from the room. Then Lust and Envy and Gluttony.

Belphegor then appeared in the centre of the temple. Everybody stood on edge, ready to pounce.

"Come here Sloth, it's time to go." Belphegor welcomed with a curly finger.

"I'm not coming." Sloth announced bravely.

"Silly man. They won't forgive your sins." Belphegor announced before grabbing Jack Frost and disappearing out of the room.

"He is right." Samuel confirmed snatching his sister out of Sloth's sweating hands. "She is the only reason I don't kill you where you stand."

Sophie hugged her brother with delight as tears streamed down both of their faces. Their reunion was short-lived as the temple began to shake its decrepitude all around them.

"We need to get out of here now before this whole place comes down on our heads. Everyone back to my place for a nice warm cup of Ovaltine?" Jasper suggested through his bloodied face.

"What about Jack? Please, we can't just leave him." The Tooth Fairy protested, crying her little heart out.

"Despite everything he's done I would do anything to go after him. I'd even give my life to save him. But we don't have a clue where he is Deanne." Rupert suggested.

"But he is one of us. He is a Festive. He just proved he is on our side." Deanne pitched as everyone else started evacuating the temple.

"He will always be one of us and I'm hoping he still has something up his sleeve to escape, but this temple is collapsing around us. We have to go now." Jasper remonstrated.

The entire group left the temple with a mix of emotions. Some were angry, some were relieved and some didn't know exactly what they were feeling.

CHAPTER 46

THE CHEST

The Six Deadly Sins took turns booting Jack Frost around the room before they grew bored and decided to finish him off.

"Don't kill him yet." Belphegor ordered as he struggled to open the small treasure chest he had obtained from the temple.

Belphegor strained and grunted as he tried to tear the trunk apart. Giving in, he began to angrily throw it against the stone walls of what appeared to be an underground castle. Frustrated, he took Pride's sword off him and tried to cut the chest open. He took one of Envy's knives off her and tried to prize it open. He took one of Lust's gloves from her and tried to pick the lock. He took Wrath's baseball bat and tried to smash the lock off. Nothing worked. The chest was impenetrable.

"Gluttony. Rip it open please." Belphegor demanded, handing the chest over.

Gluttony grabbed hold and attempted to prize the chest apart. It wouldn't budge. She adjusted herself and tried again. This time more determined than the first, yet still she couldn't open it.

"Greed, see if you can do your thing and get inside." Belphegor ordered.

Greed tried to put his hand inside the chest but his fingers touched the outside of the box preventing him. He tried again, and again and again.

"I can't do it." He finally admitted, giving in.

"Jack. How do I open this stupid thing?" Belphegor demanded, throwing it at Jack, but narrowly missing.

"I'm not telling you." Jack said with a weak giggle.

"Perhaps the threat of death can tempt you into revealing the chest's secret." Belphegor reasoned as he approached Jack.

"Death is a just reward after what I did to my best friends for you." Jack declared climbing to his feet.

"I don't mean your death silly. Sitri, go and get our final prisoner please." Belphegor said with a smile.

"Yes sir." Sitri declared before disappearing from the room.

Jack Frost looked shocked and disappointed. It annoyed him that he clearly wasn't the cleverest man in the room. Sitri quickly returned gripping hold of an emaciated man by the purple rags that he wore. The prisoner didn't have a face where an ordinary man should have one, instead he had a pumpkin head. The flame lighting up his carved face had almost diminished.

"Jack O'Lantern, you're alive." Jack Frost said, falling to his knees in shock.

"Tell us how to get into the chest or I will kill him." Belphegor threatened, grabbing Pride's sword from him and approaching the hunched figure.

"I'm really sorry Jack, but I can't tell them." Jack Frost declared to his friend.

"It's okay mate. I'm ready to die." Jack O'Lantern assured.

Belphegor stabbed Jack O'Lantern in his right shoulder. The pumpkin head screamed as the sword went through him.

"Please stop." Jack Frost pleaded as he was held in place by the Sins.

Belphegor then ran the sword through Jack O' Lantern's left shoulder. Jack Frost cried as he was held in place.

"Please don't do this. I got you the chest, didn't I?" Jack Frost pleaded.

Belphegor then pulled Jack O' Lantern's decrepit hand out from his body and lined the sword up, ready to chop it off. Jack O' Lantern couldn't look at his shaking hand any longer. He closed his eyes ready for the cut.

"Please, no." Jack Frost begged in tears as he realised what Belphegor was about to do.

"Last chance." Belphegor threatened, hovering with the sword.

Jack Frost fell deathly silent. He had stopped his pleading and his crying and his resisting. As Belphegor lifted the sword as high as he could ready to bring it down and chop off Jack O' Lantern's hand in one fell swoop, Jack Frost spoke.

"I will tell you where the key is on one condition." Jack Frost declared defeatedly.

"No. Don't do it. Don't tell 'em." Jack O' Lantern pleaded.

"Quiet fool." Belphegor announced striking Jack O' Lantern across the back of the pumpkin, knocking him out.

"What is the condition?" Belphegor enquired.

"I swear I will tell you but you have to let him go first." Jack Frost reasoned.

"He is lying. Don't trust him." Envy expostulated.

"Don't do it." Wrath pleaded.

"Silence!!!" Belphegor shouted. "Tell me where the key is and I promise I will let him go." Belphegor proposed.

"Let him go and I swear I will tell you." Jack promised.

"Fine. Sitri, take Jack O' Lantern to the same place you took Jack's sisters and then come straight back." Belphegor announced.

Sitri disappeared with the pumpkin-headed man then returned immediately. You could tell the Six Deadly Sins wanted to protest but didn't dare.

"Now. Where, is, the, key?" Belphegor asked, approaching Jack Frost and grabbing him by his neck.

"A vampire has it." Jack admitted.

"Which vampire? Where?" Belphegor quizzed, choking Jack.

"Winwood. Libra Base." Jack breathed, choking on the words.

"Good. He is yours now." Belphegor announced throwing Jack to the floor like an unwanted ragdoll.

CHAPTER 47

A FAMILY GATHERING

As the group all poured through the portal, some of their family ran over to greet them. Ollie bounced excitedly to his sister Mollie and gave her a big furry hug. Anya squeezed her father Jasper and then her Uncle Rupert before hugging her cousin Nova.

Deanne and Aoife noticed one of the little elves looking around expectantly for his friend. The fairies decided they should be the ones to tell him how brave his friend had been, and how he was the only one who had actually managed to pull any of the gems out of the door before he died. The elf was upset, but he was proud

"I will be right back. I need to grab three more guests." Sandman announced before disappearing into thin air.

Within thirty seconds he returned with a small elf and two people dressed in long yellow robes.

"Erika!" One of the small elves said excitedly, running over and hugging her.

"Oh, I totally forgot. Somebody arrived while you were all gone." Anya remembered.

"Who?" Jasper asked with intrigue.

"Why don't you go inside and have a look for yourselves."

The treetops glistened as the group made their way over to Jasper's house which looked lovely and cosy with its smoking chimney. As Anya pushed the door open and Nova walked inside, she couldn't believe her eyes. Her father Santa Claus was sitting by the fire covered in bandages, looking like an overfed mummy.

"What! How are you even alive?" Nova said, running over and hugging her Dad, completely ignoring his obvious injuries.

"Ow. Ow. Ow. Ow." He yelped before bursting into laughter.

"So, how are you... Well here?" Nova pressed.

"Well, funny story actually. I always keep twenty-five pints of blood hidden away just in case something like this ever happens. I've had to use up my full supply while I cured my injuries but, such is life." Santa explained before everyone took turns hugging him, including the people he had never met before who simply didn't want to be left out.

"So, what have I missed?" He asked merrily.

Everyone in the room took turns filling him in on every little thing that had happened since the start. Some of it was good news, some of it was bad news and some of it he couldn't quite believe.

"So, they have the chest now?" Santa asked when they had finished explaining everything.

"And Jack Frost." Deanne said, bursting into tears again.

"Don't discount the fella yet, he is a clever boy Jack is." Santa explained before reaching over and grabbing his red and white overalls. He seemed to search through both of the pockets for quite a while before he eventually plucked out what looked like a small black brick with a spike sticking out of the top. Santa pulled up the aerial making the thing even bigger.

"What the hell is that?" Anya asked with wonder.

"It's my mobile phone." Santa said with a smile.

"No wonder we can never hear you on that bloody thing. Who you ringing?" Nova asked with a giggle.

"An archangel friend of mine. His name is Cassiel." Santa explained as he began keying in the numbers.

CHAPTER 48

AS BAD AS IT GETS

On Froome Island, Jack O'Lantern was woken up by someone lightly slapping his pumpkin face. He looked up to see three girls standing over him. There was a woman in silver armour with singed black hair, a woman with a musty coat with brown knotted curls and a ginger-haired woman who looked like she had antlers coming out of her head.

"Who are you?" Jack asked weakly.

"The Seasonals. Have you seen Jack Frost?" Jennifer put in.

"He saved me. But he's gonna tell them that Winwood has the key." Jack said before passing out.

"Who the hell is Winwood and what key?" Jasmine asked.

"Not the foggiest." Jillian answered, shrugging her shoulders.

"We should take him to the other Festives. Perhaps they know." Jennifer suggested.

*****

All six of the Sins approached Jack with excitement. Pride was first, he cracked Jack over the head with the hilt of his sword then slashed his face with the blade. Jack didn't even try to fight back. He was about to get the death he felt he deserved. Envy stabbed him in both of his legs, then in the belly. As blood poured out of his wounds, Gluttony picked him up and threw him across the room. His shoulder cracked in two as he hit the stone wall with a thump.

Jack Frost struggled back to his feet. A smile spreading back across his face as Wrath ran across the room and hit his elbow with a baseball bat. The horrible crunch of the break echoed throughout the room. Wrath then did the same with the other side. Yet still, Jack Frost remained standing and ready for more. Lust then scratched his back and then his chest with her poisoned claws, before booting him across the room. Jack had to give everything he had left to get back to his feet, but he managed. He refused to die lying down.

Finally, Greed approached the smirking Festive and simply grabbed his still-beating heart and yanked it out of his body. Envy quickly snatched it off him and stabbed Jack's heart repeatedly with one of her little daggers. As Jack Frost fell toward the cold hard floor, he was hoping to see the friends he had betrayed on the other side.

In the throne room Belphegor was talking to Sitri when Greed interrupted.

"It's done Sir. Jack Frost is dead." Greed said, bending over into a kneeling position.

"Good. We are done with the annoying Festives now. You have a new mission." Belphegor informed.

"What is that master?" Greed asked excitedly.

"Find that Libra base and bring me that key." Belphegor ordered.

"What about Sloth?" Greed asked.

"Forget him, he is dead to us. Just concentrate on your new mission."

"Very well. We will get right on it." Greed suggested before standing up and leaving.

TO BE CONTINUED...

The Festives will return in...

VOLUME VIII: ANGELS AND SEASONS

The next book in the "Apocalypse Genesis" series will be.

VOLUME IV: THE COLLECTOR'S APPRENTICE

*****

For more information about myself, or the Apocalypse Genesis series, please follow me on twitter.

@JamieRichmond16

*****

Special Thanks

Firstly, let me thank my fantastic proof readers Claire, Sharon and Andrew, who kindly comb through my work and weed out the majority of my countless mistakes. Words cannot thank you enough for your brilliant help in bringing this book to print.

Secondly, let me say a huge well done and thanks to my cover illustrator Bryony Anne Ryan for helping me assemble a third book cover. To see more of what she can do or hire her yourself, please check out her website.
www.bryonyaryan.portfoliobox.net

Finally, I would like to thank Andrew Mowat (and the lovely people at the Seaview Hotel in John O'Groats) for the use of the hotels name in the book. If you're reading this and you haven't been yet, you should get packing!

Printed in Great Britain
by Amazon